MOON
WATER
MADNESS

MOON
WATER
MADNESS

by
Glynn Marsh Alam

MEMENTO MORI MYSTERIES
New York

F/a
Mys

Memento Mori Mysteries
Published by
Avocet Press Inc
19 Paul Court, Pearl River, NY 10965
http://www.avocetpress.com
mysteries@avocetpress.com

AVOCET PRESS

Library of Congress Cataloging-in-Publication Data
Alam, Glynn Marsh, 1943-
Moon water madness / by Glynn Marsh Alam. — 1st ed.
p. cm.
ISBN 978-0-9677346-4-4
1. Fogarty, Luanne (Fictitious character)—Fiction. 2. Women detectives—Florida—Tallahassee Region—Fiction. 3. Women divers—Fiction. 4. Girls—Fiction. 5. Family secrets—Fiction. 6. Tallahassee Region (Fla.)—Fiction. 7. Domestic fiction. I. Title.
PS3551.L213M66 2009
813'.54—dc22
2008035959

Printed in the USA
First Edition

To Clara, who has her own past tense.

To the reader:
There is no such place as Moon Island.
Don't even try to find it on a map.

A bull alligator is a quiet, stealthy walker in spite of his size. During mating season he shuffles forward one side at a time and will cross anything to find females. Barriers do not prevent his movement, and should a door stand open he will sneak through. His primeval claws tapping on rotting floors will be the only warning. He is especially dangerous to smallness. An unaware child is no match for his lechery. The bull gator will carry that child away to a watery stash, unless the child senses the bull's presence and outsmarts him. That is when innocence becomes deadly. That's when the bull gator never makes it to his mating nest.

CHAPTER ONE

"It'll be dark soon," Pasquin leaned back in the rocker and shut his eyes. "Might even be a full moon out. You checked the date?"

"You have to look at today's paper to know what day it is?" I asked, stretching back in my own rocker and watching two squirrels chase each other into the trees across the road from my front porch. Florida was lazy in the deep summer, the blanket of humidity covering us like an invisible veil, welcome after the May drought. I didn't wait for the old man's answer. He was rocking gently now, smiling as he pushed his straw hat over his face. "Doesn't matter if there is a full moon or not," I said. "You'd find your way home in total pitch black."

He stopped rocking. "Somebody just docked at your landing."

I stared at him. His hat covered his eyes. How did this eighty-plus old man sense a boat had pulled up to my landing that was hidden by a solid summer growth of trees?

"How do you know?"

"Heard the motor. Didn't you?"

I listened, wondering if my eardrums had gone bad. The scene in front of me sat undisturbed, until a bird flew from a bush and a young girl with the face of a time-worn woman walked from the trees onto the dirt drive in front of the house.

I stood up, letting the rocker sway against the back of my shins. In my lifetime in this swamp, I thought I knew everybody. This girl was a stranger. Her dark-circled eyes looked hollow. Her hair, long and dirty blond, lay tangled about her bony shoulders. I couldn't tell if it was wind blown or just uncombed. She looked like she needed a good meal.

She stopped suddenly when she caught my image through the screen. The toes of her ragged slip-ons hit the sandy earth and sent it flying a short distance in front of her.

"Are you Miss Luanne Fogarty?" she asked in a loud, heavy voice. She stared without blinking.

"I am," I said, wondering about the antiquated use of "Miss" before my name. I opened the screen door. She didn't budge or cross the road and mount the steps to my front porch.

"My name is Sissy Moon." She flinched slightly when she saw Pasquin rise from his rocker. He had removed his straw hat and held it at his side. "I live over the briny water on Moon Island."

"Yes," said Pasquin. "Lordy! A name out of the past. Haven't been there in years. Used to be a dock there where we could load barges."

Sissy stared at the old man, refusing to say another word.

"This is Mr. Dorian Pasquin," I said. "He lives about a half mile that way." I pointed to the path that led into the woods beside my house. "Won't you come in?"

"No ma'am," she said and shook her head. "I been sent over here to hire you out."

Behind me, I heard Pasquin chuckle and mumble that maid service must be hard to come by these days.

"Hire me out? For what?"

"My grandma says you got diving equipment and know how to swim around lake bottoms. Is that true?"

"Yes, I do that for the sheriff when he needs me."

"She's not takened to the law. Just you." Sissy began to rummage down the front of her shirt that had been tucked inside faded jeans. "Grandma said I was to give you this if you come today." She lifted out a manila envelope.

"What is it?" I said and walked down the steps.

Sissy jerked the envelope behind her. "You can't have it until you agree."

"To what?"

"Grandma said Grandpa went running to the lake and jumped himself in and never come up again. She wants you to go down there and find him and bring him back."

My slight amusement turned cold all of a sudden. I glanced back at Pasquin who stood on the top step.

"You mean he's in the lake and you didn't call the sheriff?"

Sissy shook her head. "Grandma don't taken to a sheriff. This here's half the money for coming and trying. You bring him up, you get the other half." She brought the envelope back to her front and opened it for me to see several bills inside.

"Sissy, look, I dive for the sheriff, but I really don't hire out to private parties." I stared at her face that had grown mean and cloudy. "But, maybe…"

"You gon' do it or not? I got to get back. Grandma don't taken to me on the river with all this money."

I glanced at Pasquin again. He shrugged.

"Something you got to do, Luanne. You go get the diving gear, and I'll chat with Sissy." He winked and nodded toward the living room.

Pasquin knew I kept the diving gear in the carport in a locked cabinet. I caught his drift and headed for the living room. Inside I dialed Tony Amado, sheriff's detective and the one person who would hire me if the department needed an extra scuba tank in a deep spring.

"We didn't get any calls from that way," Tony said, always ready to doubt what I said. "You sure about this?"

"No, I'm not sure about anything. This young kid says her grandpa jumped into the lake and never came up again. I don't even know if there is a lake on that island."

"Just a minute." Tony leaned away from the phone and spoke to someone. I heard the word map a few times. "Yeah," he said when he came back. "There's a deep lake on that island, right behind the big old house owned by the Moon family. And guess what the name of the lake is? Moon Lake."

"Well, it would seem that old man Moon jumped into the lake and needs rescuing. Although, if he's not up by now, we'll be rescuing a body. Look, I need to go. The kid doesn't know I called you."

"Glad you did. You go on by boat. We'll meet you there. From this map it looks like we can take a road around the mainland and cross a dinky bridge. Sure hope it holds."

"Maybe you'd best haul a boat, just in case," I said and put down the phone.

After pulling on a bathing suit with my jeans and tee-shirt over it, I moved to the back door and went around to the carport to collect the gear. I pulled the tank behind me as I followed Sissy and Pasquin to the landing.

"She's agreed to go in front of us," said Pasquin. "I'll follow in my boat with you and this stuff." I'd given him the box with a diving suit, fins and mask.

"I don't taken to going fast on the river," said Sissy when she climbed into a homemade thing with unsanded boards and a cheap motor attached to one end. "Grandma says no sense in two of us being under the water." She turned to me and handed me the envelope.

"Sissy, this isn't necessary…" I started to pass it back to her.

"We can settle that later," said Pasquin. "Keep it for now."

I leaned over and stuck it into his shirt pocket. "You be the banker."

Sissy started her motor after two tries, backed out of the space and headed for deep water. She seemed at ease with the old craft, like she had been taught and given lots of practice. Pasquin did the same and kept a few yards behind her wake as we chugged up the river. It seemed an eternity, and I figured if old man Moon needed rescuing, he would be in a state of decay by the time we arrived.

"This is just too strange, Pasquin," I said, holding onto the side of the boat as he steered it down the Palmetto River. He dodged cypress groves and areas of heavy grass, keeping pace with the young Sissy. "How old do you think she is?"

"Looks about ten, eleven," he said. "I'm trying to recall the Moon family. There used to be a big old Southern house there, but haven't heard about it many years. Not sure how many generations of Moons lived there, but a lot. And it's not really an island. Just a piece of land jutting into the bay with water on three sides." He laughed. "I recall a story of one old Moon who decided he didn't like people walking onto his land and dug, or tried to dig, the land out that connected him to the other part of the woods. Managed to make it deep enough to flood during high tide, but people could still walk across it if so inclined."

"Have you ever been to the interior?"

He shook his head. "Never needed to. We used the dock area on the bay side to tie up barges in storms and such. Not much use for anything else."

"And how did the Moons make their living? Surely, there isn't any room for farming."

"No more than a vegetable patch, I'd think." He pulled off his hat and hit the air to drive away some horse flies that had decided to hang around the moving boat. "Most people down that way made a living off the ocean—oysters, shrimp, mullet."

The river ran a good four miles before it opened to the Bay and the fresh water mixed with the salty ocean. Manatees swam here, taking advantage of the warmer currents. Signs dotted the banks and the edges of the river warning boaters to slow the engines or cut the propellers to protect the manatees. That slowed us down even more. I kept thinking about an old man struggling in lake water, maybe hanging onto a rotten log and trying to reach shore. But Sissy said Grandpa went down and never came up, which meant he'd be found stuck on an underwater limb or maybe in a day or so, he'd float to the top and his bloated body would be revealed.

Sissy waved back at us to follow her around a bend and into a lane between cypress knees, the last before the river opened into the sea. Heavy pine forests dotted the shoreline, but when Sissy rounded a narrow water lane, the river opened and there was an island, a small spot of oaks and pines, encircled by river water. She moved her boat beyond our sight. We followed and found ourselves at a dock in deep water.

"Ideal for small boats to tie up here," said Pasquin. He pulled the boat near the dock and flung the rope over a post. "Big boats have to use the other side. Don't suppose they have any need to do that anymore."

"How come I don't know these people?" I steadied myself in the rocking boat before climbing onto the aged wood of the dock. Someone had repaired it in spots, the new nails reflecting the sunlight like diamonds in raw lumber roughness.

"Not much to know since the old ones died off, and the young ones left. Maybe shrimp boats tie up here now." Pasquin chuckled as he fanned himself with his hat. "And I'll bet not too many of those. People like the Moons isolate themselves, don't want contact with the public."

"And that's why the old lady would rather hire me than call the sheriff?"

We trudged up a narrow sand path until the pine trees grew tall and the oaks canopied our route. The overhanging limbs and heavy moss darkened the way, making Sissy's skinny body almost disappear at times.

"Maybe she chucked the old guy in herself," Pasquin stopped at the edge of the trees. "Look at that old thing!"

He wasn't aiming his finger at Sissy's grandma but at a house that must have been a beacon of grandeur in its day. With upstairs and downstairs wrap-around porches, it had once been painted snow white to deflect the sun's rays. Now it was nearly the color of the tree trunks around it. On one corner, the upstairs porch sagged. It would be treacherous to step on that end, but someone had tried to bolster the middle and opposite ends with new beams and more raw boards. I wondered if they did the same around back.

Sissy climbed the wide steps in front and shucked her shoes on the porch. The boards looked old and worn, but she didn't seem to worry about splinters. The screen door slammed behind her.

"I guess we wait here," I said. "No one seems to be in any hurry to fish out poor Grandpa."

"He'd be drowned by now anyway," said Pasquin. He frowned and seemed preoccupied with the scrub trees that surrounded the house.

"Sure is quiet out here," he said.

"The lake is supposed to be in the back?" I moved to the corner of the porch to look beyond the front. I saw nothing but more scrub brush, high trees, and the hint of an old shed.

Before we moved further into the rear of the yard, voices came from the dark space where the screen door sat uneven with the frame. Sissy's high pitch was obvious but the male voice was new.

"You people needn't be here," said a man with dirty jeans and no shirt. He slammed open the screen door where it stuck on a warped floor and showed no inclination to shut against him. His thin red hair with flecks of gray lay damp against his bloated face. He had the ruddy and sweaty skin of someone who worked outside. "That old lady is half out of her mind."

"Do you mean no one fell into a lake—or even jumped in?" I asked.

"It's an old family tale." His voice boomed with anger. "Been told for years that my grandpa went into the lake and never came out."

"Then who's her grandpa?" Pasquin pointed to a defiant Sissy. She had moved to one side of the porch and stood with her hands on her hips.

"The man who supposedly went into the lake is her great-grandpa. We just call him grandpa because her real one takened up and left before she was born. Far as I'm concerned, he don't exist."

In the distance a boat siren wailed through the trees. Pasquin and I both turned to face the trail, unable to see the water through the forest.

"Look, sir, the sheriff is on his way." I gave Sissy an apologetic shrug. "If someone is reported in the water and maybe drowned,

I have to call the law. They'd have me in jail if I just dived for the money and didn't report it." I turned to the man again. "Surely, you must realize this."

The man took a deep breath. His big body nearly folded into itself. His face looked to be the result of a thousand genetic mistakes. He sat in a rocker whose runners matched the aged boards on the floor.

"She offered to pay you?" He put his head in his hands and sat silent for a moment. When he lifted his face, his anger had gone. "She's got some kind of dementia, you see. Things from the past come creeping up in the canals of her brain and pop out every once in a while." He put his face back in his hands. "You have no idea."

"Just who are we talking about?" asked Pasquin.

The man rested his elbows on his knees. "Mrs. Beatrice Moon, my grandma, Sissy's great grandma, the matriarch of the Moon family."

"And you are?"

"Corwin Moon, her grandson." He looked up when the first sheriff's deputy stepped out of the tree line. He didn't bother getting up. "And the kid's Pa."

Pasquin and I stood still until three deputies, one of them Vernon Drake, and Tony Amado stood at the porch line.

"Where's the lake?" Amado asked me.

"I suppose around back. But there doesn't seem to be a problem after all." I grinned and shrugged. Tony wasn't going to let this one drop for a long time.

The men looked at each other. One of the deputies finally smiled and said, "Sure glad we didn't drag the diving equipment down that path."

Vernon turned to look at the trees, smiling. He knew the frustration of being called out on a nonexistent problem. It was something that rattled a lot of his colleagues, but he had learned to take it with humor. Tony, on the other hand, still let it burn beneath his well-pressed collar.

"Is this a nuisance call?" He looked at me then quickly turned to Mr. Moon.

"Sorry, sir, but my old grandma takened it into her head that Grandpa needed fishing out of the lake and sent my daughter off to hire this lady here." Corwin Moon stood up and came to the top step. He looked directly at me. "I'm assuming she gave you some money?"

I looked at Pasquin. "He's holding it. It's not something I do, you know. That's why I called the sheriff." I nodded to Pasquin. He fished out the envelope and planned to pass it to Mr. Moon.

"No! That belongs to Grandma!" Sissy ran and snatched it from Pasquin's hand and darted inside the door. We could hear her feet slapping against the stairs as she made her way up to the next floor and, most likely, the old lady.

Tony paced while the deputies wiped the humidity from their faces. "I can't just go away without finding out something," he said. "You fellows have a seat." He motioned the men to the porch. "Luanne, you come with me."

I followed him up the steps and toward the door. Corwin Moon stood aside, surprised and not knowing what to do.

"I want to see this old lady, sir."

Corwin stared a moment, his eyes angry and defiant, but they soon turned to resignation and he said, "Follow me."

An air of shabby decay greeted us inside the dark living room. A coffee table sat piled with various books, their titles unreadable in the dim light. The staircase was directly in front of the door at the end of a hall. Before we could risk the old boards, steps came heavily, followed by the barefoot slaps of the girl.

"I told her you made her give the money back!" Sissy screamed at her father. "She ain't none too happy about that." It was threatening talk, not the kind you often heard from young Southern girls from old families.

"Oh, take her back up," said Corwin and backed toward a tattered sofa. He sat down and stared at the woman who held on to the railing and hit each step with feet clad in huge orthopedic shoes. Thick ankles rested atop the sides of the shoes. She wore opaque socks. Above that were legs skinny enough to be skeleton bone.

At the bottom step she stopped so suddenly that her great-grandchild bumped her lightly from behind.

"I paid my money for this!" She pointed at Corwin. "You will not go against my wishes. And I wish my husband to be found!" The voice was an older version of Sissy's, gruff and loud. She lowered her thin arm and reached around, taking hold of Sissy's shoulder. "You show them the lake, girl." She gave a slight push, moving the girl to the front, but keeping a grip on the shoulder. "I may be nearly 100 years old, but I ain't takened crazy yet." Her eyes watered now, big and bright in a face that wasn't nearly as skinny as the rest of her. The thin hair had been circled into a kind of bun behind her neck. It may have been white, but her freckled skin and blue eyes made me suspect it had been bright red at one time.

"Why do you say your husband fell into the lake?" asked Tony.

"He didn't fall! He jumped in and never came up. Something takened him down there."

"And when did this happen?"

"1959," she said and went silent.

CHAPTER TWO

Tony looked around him and frowned at the ill-kept room. It occured to me that dealing with the elderly was not his strongest point. I stepped in front of him.

"What makes you think we can find him now?" I asked.

"He never came out, and I heard him down there. Keep hearing him every time I go to the edge." She raised her arm again and shook her finger at me. "And don't say I'm loony. You need to go down there and look for yourself."

"Mrs. Moon," I said, moving closer to the stairs. "Could you or your grandson sit down and tell us just what happened?"

She straightened up and let go of the rail. Brushing the front of her cotton dress, she headed for the sofa and sat at the other end from Corwin. She motioned for Tony and me to use the other chairs. There were four to choose from, all threadbare and musty.

"I shall tell you a bit, but then I'm going to show you," she said. Her voice had turned into the grand old lady inflections of someone about to serve lemonade on the porch. "Sissy will come along to help." The young girl had taken up a position at the end of the sofa behind the old lady. She stood like a sentinel and glared at Corwin.

"I takened Oscar Moon for a husband when I was only sixteen," she said. "He lived in this grand old house and had a business dealing with fishermen who went way out to sea."

Tony sighed as though we were in for a long haul of a tale.

"'Tweren't easy being married to an older man. I gave him three babies that lived, but he weren't all that grateful." Her eyes flashed for a moment. "Two was girls and he wanted boys. He finally got one. The baby. Gave that boy everything. He married a ship slut and gave us this." She waved an old hand toward Corwin who scowled back at her. "Then he ups and marries another ship slut…"

"Grandma!" Sissy whispered in the old lady's ear.

"Yes, child." She patted the girl's hand that rested on her shoulder.

"Get to the part about Grandpa."

"Things turned bad with his son. Couldn't trust him and that woman. One day, both just takened themselves off somewhere and we never saw a hair on their bodies again—at least not hers. We seen him in jail a few times 'fore he died. Now his young'n is in the same jail."

"His young'n?" Tony nodded toward Corwin.

"Not him. His brother Aaron."

"Grandpa had men around to help him," said Corwin defiantly.

"Married to our daughters," the old lady nodded. "Could have worked out but they both takened to drink. Both left and took my daughters away." She waved a hand in front of her. "But I'm getting away from the main story."

"You always do," said Corwin, "when it comes to your precious daughters."

"Your aunts!"

"My aunts," he shook his head.

Tony shifted forward. "Ma'am, your husband?"

"Just got frustrated one day," she said. "I was upstairs and he slammed down here and out the door. Heard him yell he was going to the lake." She sat still and stared into the stale room air. For a moment, she seemed to lose the thought. "I was near the back window up there," she pointed to the top floor. "I heard him hollering about something. Heard a splash. This time I knew he was in trouble. By the time I takened the stairs and run around back, he was nowhere in sight."

The room sat silent for a moment, until Corwin gave a slight sneer. "So it is told."

"How do you know it's not true?" Sissy held tight to the lady's shoulder and nearly yelled at her father. "Were you here?"

Corwin smiled and shook his head but said no more.

"Did anyone try and find him?" asked Tony.

"He's still there," said Mrs. Moon, shaking her head and letting her eyes glaze over again. She stared into the room and didn't come out of the stupor this time.

"Aw! Take her to her room," Corwin yelled at the girl.

Sissy moved to the front of her grandma and gently pulled on her arm. The lady glanced her way, stood and trudged up the stairs, deflated as though the fire had left her soul.

"She's senile," said Corwin. "That story pops up every now and then. One day, she caught some young kids swimming around in that lake and asked them to look for her husband. Scared them to death. They takened to the shore and never came back."

"What young kids?" asked Pasquin. "I didn't know anyone else lived on this island."

"Don't," said Corwin. "But seems everybody's got a boat and getting here is easy."

A yell came from the top of the stairs. "We got boarders living here!" It was Sissy whose ears weren't out of range yet.

"Yeah, yeah," said Corwin. "We rent out rooms by the night or week, once in a while a whole month, to fish boat crews. Don't charge much. Just make it convenient."

"And are there any boarders here now?" asked Tony. He moved to the bottom of the stairs and stared upward.

"Got two, but they're out on boats. Expect them later, after dark."

"Who does the meals for them?" I asked. I couldn't see the old lady capable and surely Sissy was too young.

"Nobody. See, we tell them up front. Food is in the cupboards and refrigerator. You do your own. It's kind of an honor system."

He looked up and smiled. "They come and go, see. And when I'm not here, they rent from the old lady. She keeps the bills."

I wondered how an old lady with limited mental capacity could be trusted to collect money for rooms. She seemed feisty enough not to let anyone cheat her, but could she always remember what was owed? I figured young Sissy was called to duty more often than not.

Tony sat silent for a moment, then nodded for me to follow him outside.

"Mr. Moon," he turned toward Corwin, "wait for us here, please."

We stood at the bottom of the stairs, soaked in the humid air and slapped off bugs whose presence was shown only by their bites. Tony frowned and spoke to Vernon and me.

"Look, we've had some embarrassments before when we thought we were dealing with loonies, but it turned out there was really something there." He took a deep breath. "I don't like this, but we better make at least a partial dive in that lake."

"We'll have to go back to the boat to suit up," said Vernon. He pinched my elbow as though saying "See what you've made us do?"

"Look," I said and stared at Tony while nudging Vernon's rib cage, "Let's ask if we can use a room in the house to suit up. That way, we can get a look without a search warrant."

Tony's face went stiff then broke into a half smile. "Deviousness becomes you, Luanne." He pointed toward the porch. "I'll get permission."

"You're wantin' to do what?" said Corwin, his red face turning purple.

"We have to check things out, sir," said Tony. "We must since a report was made that someone was in the lake. Now, we can suit up here or at our boat. I'm just asking for a room for the divers to put on their suits."

"And I suppose you'll splash water all over these here rotten boards when you get out?"

"No, sir," I said. "We'll walk straight back to the boat in the suits."

Corwin looked at me, something registering in his faded eyes. "I ain't paying you."

"Taxes will pay her and everyone else," said Tony. "Your grandma can keep her envelope."

Corwin stood and hiked his dirty jeans. He nodded for us to follow him to a room across from the kitchen.

"Used to be storage for home canned goods, but don't nobody know how to do that anymore. 'Cept Grandma but she'd burn the place down if she tried."

"Not much room in here," Vernon smiled. "Guess we'll have to take turns."

"You weren't planning on dressing together?" Corwin's red face went nearly pale.

"No sir," said Vernon who winked at me. "Ladies first." He made a half bow and let me in the room about the size of two closets. "I'll tell Pasquin to bring in the suit."

While the other deputies carried the tanks to the bank of the river, I stripped down and pulled on the wet suit. I figured I could dive with only a bathing suit but who knew what was in that lake. Better to cover up the skin. Pulling the cord to turn on the bare bulb, I looked around the room before disrobing, hoping no one could peep through the flimsy boards. Shelves that had once held jars of fruit preserves and peas sat full of dust and spider webs. Some boxes that looked fairly new rested in one corner. I used them as a balance since they appeared to be sturdier than the walls. On top of one shelf, a short stack of yellowing newspapers sat as though someone planned to use them for something one day. The place smelled damp and rancid, like long dead rats.

"All yours," I said to Vernon as I exited with fins and mask in my hand.

Corwin stood in the kitchen and nearly dropped his cup when he saw me appear in the wet suit. He said nothing, but who knows what was running through that brain. It was the suit that startled him. I'd seen it before. I guessed I looked only half human to him.

Vernon joined me, and Corwin stared until we headed out the door, then he followed us to the lake.

"It's through those trees," he said. "Only one side of it is good for swimming. That's where the kids come ever now'n then to swing on the vines, and…" He ran out of words.

"We've dived in lots of 'no swimming' places," said Vernon. "How deep is the lake?"

Corwin shrugged. "Never measured it. Deep enough in spots. Never swam in it."

"You never even put a canoe on it?" I asked.

"Nope. Never had one. I did see one years ago. Don't remember whose."

"You ever fish here?" Vernon stood at the end of the trees and stared at the expanse of the lake.

"Have sometimes. Can't tell Grandma where we got the fish 'cause she don't want nothing that could have nibbled off Grandpa." He laughed. "We tell her the fish came from the ocean. Most times they did."

We checked the tanks and donned masks with headlights attached. We entered the water on the side where Corwin said swimmers stayed. It was clear here, with a white sandy bottom, but soon dropped off, and our suspicions were confirmed that this was a sinkhole. If Grandpa had gone into it on the other side, he may not have made it out. An old man trying to swim across to the shallow section may have just given out and drowned. His body could well have drifted far down into a passage and stuck there.

Vernon and I nodded after planning our movements and walked into the water. Warm at first, it cooled rapidly from an aquifer somewhere deep, maybe more than one. I made a mental note to find out if any cave divers had explored this lake.

The sinkhole sides were like many we'd been in before, lined with tree limbs and vines, some attached by roots and some broken and rotting atop others in the water. It was unsafe to swim into this tangled mess. We moved around the edges, shining the lights onto the sides first and then into the depths. When nothing showed up along the sides, we moved through water that seemed clear and cold in the center until we came to one side of the swimming area. Here, the white sand became an underwater bank that sloped off for nearly five feet, then opened to a limestone cave. Some debris lay near the sides of the opening, but mostly it was clear, and big enough for both of us to enter. From the sides, we felt cold aquifer water shooting upward. It flowed outward, toward the center of the lake. The water pushed stray tree limbs back. A few feet away, the bottom turned downward abruptly into a narrow opening. Obviously, the cave was deep and went somewhere. We were police divers and weren't about to find out where.

"The opening is large enough for a body to fit through," I said as a deputy took my tank, "but it would probably have to be pushed. The current flows against anything going down there."

Vernon shook his head as he removed the masks. "Nothing down there now. If an old man went in and never came out, I doubt he's going to now—not even his bones."

"And 1959 is a long time ago," said Tony, his sarcasm expressing more frustration that anything else.

Corwin leaned against a tree. He had grabbed a soda from somewhere and was guzzling it down. He grinned when he heard Vernon say there wasn't anything down there.

"Told you it was an old legend," he said. "Most likely, the old man just got tired of that old woman and took off. Maybe he did drown somewhere. In the ocean, I'd say. He fished out there. Liked his rum."

"The girl," said Tony, looking toward the house, "does she go to school?"

"Fall time, yep. It's summer now. She's home." Corwin took the last drop of soda and tucked the empty bottle into his waist band. "Home schooled on the mainland by a cousin."

"We'll write a report, sir," said Tony.

Vernon and I trudged back to the boats while the deputies carried the tanks. I climbed into Pasquin's boat. He had spent most of the diving time sitting on the steps at the house.

"Little Sissy says she's coming for a visit," he chuckled. "Says she hasn't talked enough to you."

"I can imagine the tales she'll tell," I said and climbed into the seat. "Get this thing on the open river." I waved to Vernon as he moved away in the back of the police boat.

Pasquin pulled out, his motor chugging into the river and keeping a slow pace until we passed the manatee signs. He eased a little then, fanning his dripping face with his hat.

"Nutty family," he said.

The wet suit was getting uncomfortable. I motioned for him to try and keep the boat under the overhang of trees.

"What makes them talk the way they do?" I asked. "They say *takened* instead of *took*."

"Just an old way of talking, I guess. Not too educated. Probably got a lot of Bible influence." Pasquin laughed and slapped his thigh with his hat. "Woman! You're the linguist. You tell me."

"I will," I said. I expected to head to my office at the university where I spent the fall and winter months teaching linguistics. I was doing the place a favor and teaching a full summer load this year. The classes had long become routine and unstimulating. Maybe finding out what was going on in the little Moon dialect would spark some new interest.

"Poor kid," I said. "There wasn't even a TV in that house, at least not one downstairs. I didn't see a phone line, either. Maybe the father has a cell."

Pasquin reached my landing and sat in a rocker for another hour, until my swamp dog, Plato, came dragging in full of sandspurs. He flopped on the porch and let the old man's hands scratch his ears. I brought out a large beef bone I'd bought for him and he took it gently in his mouth as though it was a diamond ready to be cut.

"Sun's almost gone. Better get this old body home." Pasquin rose and grunted down the steps as he'd done for more summers than I could count. I stood on the bottom step and waved as he disappeared through the trees to his boat. Even if the sun went all the way down and it wasn't a full moon, he'd find his way. It was the next thing to instinct with him.

I watched Plato lying flat on his stomach, his front paws holding down the bone while he gnawed. Whatever meat had been there was gone now and it was simply the pleasure of grinding teeth against bone. I had cooled off from a quick shower after removing the wet suit and sipping iced tea with Pasquin. Watching both Plato and the light fade behind the trees, turning them black, gave me a sense of safety, as though the world had made it through another day. A tiny frog took advantage of the failing light to hop across the road toward my house and disappear beneath the steps. I leaned my elbows back on the next step and closed my eyes. The sounds of night would begin soon, frogs and crickets and owls. I sat like this until I heard Plato give a slight airy "woof" and twigs broke near me.

"Where in the world…?" I stared at Sissy Moon. She stood like an evening ghost across the dirt drive.

"I got to talk to you," she said.

"Are you alone?"

She nodded. "Grandma said I could come. I didn't tell Corwin. He wouldn't like it."

"It's dangerous to be out on the river in the dark, Sissy. Why would you want to anger your father and come here anyway?"

The girl looked down the dirt drive as though someone could sneak up and listen. Satisfied nothing was coming, she crossed the road and stood in front of me. Plato came close and sniffed her feet and hands. She let him lick her fingers.

"That your hound?" she said.

"Yes. And do you have a pet?"

She shook her head. "Corwin don't allow no pets, specially dogs. He says they bark too much."

"Not even a hunting dog?"

"Not even," she said and watched as Plato grew bored and returned to his bone.

"Okay, Sissy, let's sit on the porch and you can talk to me."

I led her to a rocking chair, wondering how I was going to contact her father, and wondering further how I could placate his anger. Something about him frightened me, even though Sissy had no qualms about talking back to him.

"You got any supper?" She asked like a young girl who had never been taught manners, but then I guessed she could have been awfully hungry.

"Sit there," I led her to a kitchen table and motioned to a dining chair. "I'll warm up some soup and we'll have ham sandwiches with it. Okay?"

She nodded and smiled for the first time since I'd met her.

"You'd best run into the bathroom first and wash those hands." I showed her the downstairs half bath and left her soaping her hands and arms in the fashion of someone who worked the fields. When she returned to the dining table, her face was scrubbed as well.

"Your grandma teach you to wash your arms and hands before eating?"

She shook her head. "Taught me to wash both when I helped shucking oysters. I'm good at it, but oyster juice is kind of stinky."

I placed the soup in front of her and the sandwich on the side. She didn't touch it until I sat down with mine.

"Go ahead and eat," I said.

She sat with her hands in her lap and looked up at me from a nodded head. "You saying the blessing?"

"Oh," I said, embarrassed. Although it was a habit in many households, it wasn't in mine. "You say it."

I regretted that order. Sissy went on and on about how grateful we were for the food and the river and the safety of another day. When she finally asked that the food nurture us and not make us sick, she had one open palm in the air and her face turned toward heaven—eyes closed, of course.

"Amen," she said and picked up the spoon.

"Now, Miss Moon, what is it you wanted to talk to me about?"

She put down the half sandwich and wiped her fingers on a napkin. For such an unsophisticated little country girl, she had surprisingly decent table manners.

"My grandma is scared," she said.

"About what?"

"She says she gave up on Grandpa years ago, but he's come back—or his spirit has."

"Do you believe that?"

She nodded. "I didn't at first. Corwin says she's takened to crazy in the head, but she hasn't done that."

"How do you know? Has she seen a doctor?"

She shook her head. "Won't go." She picked up her sandwich and ate a few more bites before taking in more spoons of soup.

"Then why don't you believe she's crazy in the head, as your father says?"

"He lies. Told us he goes on shrimp boats sometimes, but the last time he was supposed to be out'n the Gulf, he ended up in Jacksonville, way the other side of the state."

"Did he tell you this?"

"Nope. One of his fishing buddies did. Said they'd arrested Uncle Aaron for stealing from a little store."

"And he called you to tell you Aaron was in jail?"

She looked at me and frowned as though I were an imbecile. "Of course not! We got no phone, anyhow. Corwin called a man he works with on a ship. He had to wire some money."

It all sounded rather confusing but I let it go. Vernon could check out who was in jail and what the charges were. More intriguing was why Sissy called her father by his first name. I'd heard that some people did that, even once had a little classmate who did it, but it sounded foreign to me.

"Okay. Now tell me why you don't believe your grandma is just having a brain attack about this grandpa in the lake incident."

"Cause I heard him myself," she whispered.

CHAPTER THREE

"You heard your dead grandpa?" I put down the spoon, wondering if I were dealing with a great granddaughter who had inherited more than a dialect from her relatives.

"Uh-huh. Twice in one night."

"And what did you hear him say?"

Sissy chewed on the ham and bread and twisted her face as though it were tough or maybe she had a toothache.

"Not what you'd call words exactly," she said after she swallowed her food. "More like breathy sounds that were trying to make words."

"Breathy sounds?" I searched my brain for sounds like that on the water. The river itself could make soft, sometimes eerie, noises when the tide was in and it lapped against overhanging tree branches. If waves gently pushed against the shore between fallen limbs, it could make a whispering sound, but you'd have to stand pretty quietly to hear it. "Are you sure it's not some natural sound, an animal or water currents?"

She shook her head and finished her soup. I offered her more, but she said, "No, ma'am, thank you."

"It's like this," she said. "One night we heard this big old sigh outside in the dark, kind of like a semi tire when you let the air out." She stared at me as if to ask had I ever heard such a sound. I nodded.

"Me and Grandma were sitting upstairs that time. Couldn't sleep for the heat and our fans weren't doing the job. She was telling me about her school when she was a girl, when the big sigh just swooped over the island."

"Did you investigate?"

"I looked out the window and saw some sparkles on the lake top. When I told Grandma, she sat up straight and yelled, 'It's him!' Liked to scared me to death."

"I'll bet. And how many of these big sighs did you hear that night?"

"No more. Not that night nor 'nother. But we heard the little sighs, and they sounded like words." Sissy had been toying with a few bread crusts on her plate. She stopped and looked up at me, smiling.

"You didn't really believe they were from a ghost, did you?"

She smiled again. "No, but I can't find no reason for them, and they are real. It's driving my grandma crazier than ever. Corwin might put her in a home."

"He must hear them, too."

She shook her head. "Says he's sound asleep. Hears nothing."

I stared at this waif of a child, stuck on an island years behind the rest of the world, speaking a dialect born from isolation, and being schooled away from the mainstream. Did she have a chance anywhere outside her world?

"What do you want me to do about this?" I hesitated to ask, knowing she was going to pull me into something—as Tony would say—that was none of my business.

"Grandma wants you to stay overnight, but I don't. It's not possible long as Corwin is there."

"No, he wouldn't like it." I had no desire to tangle with red-faced Corwin.

"He's not around a lot. Goes out to the shrimp boats on jobs for days." She nibbled on the last of the crumbs.

"He works on shrimp boats?"

"Says so." Sissy's coyness belied her age. Had I not been in front of her I'd say she was nearing forty. "We got two boarders right now, but Grandma says you could sleep in my room and I'd stay in Corwin's."

"He wouldn't be angry?"

"Wouldn't know." She shrugged.

"Who are your boarders?"

"Well," she took a deep breath, "there's Patel. He's a dark fellow who messes up the kitchen and sometimes sleeps on the porch. He takened his mattress and flopped out there once when it was real hot. If he's not working on a boat, he walks around in his pajamas half the day."

"Is he from India? Patel is an Indian name."

"He says he's Indian, but Grandma says he ain't no Seminole. He talks kind of strange." She smiled.

I'd seen Indians hire out on boats. Seeing one on the boats in this part of the Gulf was rare.

"And there's Trukee. I don't think that's his real name, but Grandma says it don't matter. Long as he pays his room rent and don't burn down the place."

"Is he foreign, too?"

"He's an old guy, got long gray hair and a bad face. I don't take to him much. He drinks beer, smokes, and stares at the sunset."

"How long have they rented rooms from you?"

"They come in last month and plan on staying till end of the season." She looked up at me, and it gave me pause to wonder if social services should allow a child to be around these characters day and night.

"Would you like some dessert?" I asked, figuring she needed it.

Sissy smiled and held up her sandwich plate. I cut a piece of cheesecake baked by the local grocery and handed her a fork.

"What's this?" She said and stared at the creamy concoction.

"Cheesecake. Don't you like it?"

"Never had cake made out of cheese."

"It's cream cheese. Try it."

Sissy dipped the tip of a fork into the top of the cake and tasted it. Her eyebrows shot up and she ate with gusto a delicacy she'd never seen in that decrepit house on her island.

"Look, Sissy, I don't think you should take off in that boat and head home in the night. Maybe you could sleep here and go home in the morning?" I took a deep breath when I said this. It would mean finding clean clothes and inviting a scrutiny of my privacy I might not be ready to give.

"Oh, no!" she said. "I got to get on home. Grandma can't be left alone overnight." She ate the last of the cheesecake and wiped her mouth.

"Then, wait a moment, okay." I went to the living room and called Pasquin. He was a late night person, but might be one gruff old man if I asked him to pull out the boat again. I decided to risk it.

"Look, she won't stay here and I can't send her back down the river alone. If anything happened to her, guess who'd be charged?"

"All right, woman," said Pasquin. "Meet me on the landing."

I returned to Sissy who had returned to the bathroom and was washing her hands again. She came out wiping her face on the hand towel. "I guess I got to go."

"Look," I said. "Pasquin is coming in his boat and we'll follow you home."

"No need," she said. "I'm out there all the time. I'm not scared."

"It will give me a chance to move around your island and see if I hear those sighs. Besides, if you want me to help you, you've got to start listening to the letter of the law—like underage kids can't be sent off alone on a river at night, or any other time."

I walked her to the dock and waited for Pasquin's light.

"You going to spend the night with us?"

"No. Like you said, your father is there. I'll figure out another way."

I wasn't going to tell her I planned to discuss this with Vernon and Pasquin and the dreaded Tony. He would laugh and tell me I should leave the hermits alone. When I presented him with the child neglect part, he'd wear a scowl and saunter off in a huff. It would also keep him awake until he found a solution.

We sat in the dark on the landing, watching the small boat light become larger as Pasquin traveled at just above a drift.

"Who is your home school teacher?" I asked.

"My Aunt Rachel," she said. "I just call her aunt 'cause I'm so young."

"Rachel Moon?"

"Yeah. She's my grandfather's cousin. My real grandfather, not the one in the lake."

"She must be a little old to be teaching."

"I guess. She used to teach in the county grammar school, but she gets a pension now. Got her own business."

"I see." It was a case of a retired teacher doing home school-ing. The laws seemed a bit lax, but I guess a grand-niece or third cousin would qualify as family, and the woman's teaching creden-tials were probably still good. "Does she know about the sighs?"

I felt strange calling some mysterious natural sound a sigh, but it was best to play along with Sissy.

"I told her once. She said the Moons were crazy, 'specially the ones living on the island."

"She has never lived there, then?"

"Nope." Sissy stood up as Pasquin pulled close to the dock and tossed the rope over the post.

"You ladies need to appreciate an old man," he said. "I brought along Edwin 'cause he was in my living room when you called. We could've had a good card game going." He chuckled. Edwin played at playing cards. His love was snakes and their skins, and his brain capacity was for that only. Cards wouldn't be something he could ever master no matter how many games Pasquin made him play.

"Evenin'." He saluted like a sailor, laying his hand alongside his hair that moved in several directions atop his head. It amazed me that plenty of young men wore this very same style using glop to hold it in all those places.

"I'll ride with Sissy until we get to her dock." I moved behind her to her boat.

At first she seemed a bit reluctant to let me get in, but finally pushed a towel off the seat behind her own. It was the only other place to sit. Someone had rigged a cut-in-half bench into this boat to make seats.

Sissy stood at the throttle and pushed the tiller with her fragile body, sometimes using both hands to maneuver around a cypress knee. A grown person would have steered from a seated position, but Sissy needed her stance to use all her strength. I bit my lip and let her do the steering.

"You know this river well," I said. "Even at night you know where the barriers are." I was being nice. I shuddered to think if she were alone and hit a floating log, turning the boat over and dumping her into gator feeding territory. "Can you swim?"

"Nope. Grandma said wasn't lady-like to go in swimming."

I hadn't heard that kind of thinking in many years. Somehow, modern concepts of women must not have reached Moon Island.

"Here. You hold the spotlight." She handed me a bright light rigged to a battery and told me to aim it at the water in front of the boat. Pasquin had a similar one in his boat but it was attached to a pole. Both were bright enough to light up wide patches of river. Pasquin's had the required identity red and green lights on each side of the bow and the white one on the back. So did Sissy's, but hers were rigged, not installed. Someone had done quite a job with a piece of wood and a motor.

At night, the ride seemed interminable. I tried concentrating on the areas I knew well and was surprised at how many houses and landings had gone up in the past years. During the day, they were camouflaged by the growth on the banks, but at night, their lights reflected off the water, casting the shadow of encroaching pollution.

We moved under the bridge that led to briny water and the manatees. It wouldn't be long before we'd be near the bay and on our way to the island. Up to this point, we hadn't noticed another boat on the water, except for the slow putt-putts of Pasquin behind us. When we left the lights of the classy vacation houses on the briny water shore and headed for open waters, we saw boat lights, pinpoints of red and green heading our way.

"Boat ahead," I said.

Sissy said nothing, but turned her boat toward a grove of trees and pulled under the overhanging branches. Pasquin followed, most likely questioning the sanity of letting a little girl be the leader of three grown-ups.

"Shut the lights!" she said. She clicked something and turned off her own boat lights, including the spotlight I held. Pasquin started to say something, but I waved him quiet and he turned off his lights.

The boat in the distance went its way through the water toward the inland bridge. It moved slowly, its pilot standing inside a cabin where an overhead beam gave him enough light to turn the wheel. In the back, where a rich man's yacht would have carried women who sunbathed in bikinis, this boat held a dark tarp, covering square shapes beneath it.

"Goods delivery," said Sissy and waited until the boat was around a bend. She put on the light again and moved into the water.

"What was that all about?" I asked.

"Nothing," she said. "I just stay clear of the big boats. They don't see you sometimes and can run you over."

"Have you ever been run over?" I couldn't imagine any responsible boater deliberately pushing a small boat over in the water. "I mean it might wreck the big boat, too."

"I never been run over, but I did see it happen one time. And the big boat didn't stop."

"How old are you?"

"Twelve," she said.

For twelve years on this earth, this kid had seen a lot to wise her up to her world.

Sissy finally cut the engine and let her boat drift to the tie-up at Moon Island. She had cut all the lights before we actually tied up, and Pasquin did the same. Pasquin moved his boat to another tie-up and offered to watch as I escorted Sissy to the house.

"You can't see nothing from here," she said. "I know the path pretty good by now."

"I see a light through the trees. Isn't that your house?" I said.

"Yeah, but you might get lost coming back here."

"Okay, let's sit here in the quiet for a moment and listen for this sigh you've been hearing."

She glanced toward Pasquin and sat on the bank. I sat beside her and stayed as quiet as possible. Pasquin waved his hat back and forth to ward off mosquitoes, while Edwin gazed about the banks. I assumed he was watching for water moccasins, and I wasn't sure he'd shout a warning before bagging one. He didn't have any equipment on him, but some of the stuff at his feet would make do as far as he was concerned. I shuddered to think I might ride home with a live moccasin in a bag at my feet.

"Who's that?" Edwin suddenly spoke in a loud whisper. He pointed to the top of the bank. "Somebody's up there."

We all turned to stare at what seemed to be darkness. At one spot, the darkness moved slightly. It wasn't a bush.

"Patel!" Sissy shouted, causing Pasquin to jump and make wakes around his boat.

"Miss Sissy, I've been waiting for you to come home." The darkness stood and walked into the bright spotlight that Pasquin shined toward it. The man was short and wore a dark shirt and pants, both worn and stained. His swarthy skin blended with the clothes and did not reveal his body until he was near the water. "Your grandma took off and we can't find her."

CHAPTER FOUR

"I'll circle the island in the boat. You go help Sissy look at the house," said Pasquin. "You got your phone?"

Pasquin meant I should call the sheriff. A missing woman with possible dementia was no trifling matter.

"No! Don't call," said Sissy. "She's done this before." She turned to Patel who stared at the girl. "Where's Corwin?"

"He's not here," said Patel. "He left before dark. Told Trukee he'd be back around midnight."

Sissy clenched her teeth and balled up fists at her side. "He's gone out drinking." Without another word, she turned toward the house. Taking off in a trot, she yelled back at her boarder. "Have you searched the house?"

Patel sighed and said, "It didn't happen like that, Miss. She came downstairs where I was reading and took off. She had a suitcase and was dressed in one of those old frocks she has."

Sissy stopped. "Did she say anything?"

"Nothing. Just stomped out the door and down the steps. Disappeared into the night. Trukee was on the porch, but he was smoking and just kind of laughed."

Sissy turned to me. "Trukee says he smokes regular cigarettes. Ha!"

I took that to mean he smoked weed. Since no one all the way up to Grandma liked to see the law around, it was the perfect place.

"Patel," I said, "would you sit on the back porch? I assume Trukee is still on the front. If Mrs. Moon shows up, give some kind of signal."

"A *whooooeee* usually works," Pasquin yelled in his high pitched signal that worked better than any alarm in the swamp. He revved the engine and guided his boat slowly around the tie-ups to water deep enough to allow him to circle the island in most places. Edwin sat clinging to the side of the boat, the human dilemma completely foreign to him.

Patel half ran to the house, chuckling and making low *whooooeee* sounds to himself. We heard him trying to explain to Trukee what to do if Mrs. Moon came back. There was no response we could hear, and I was afraid the man wouldn't know if Swamp Foot walked up and asked for a light.

"Let's make a circle and pass by the lake," I said. Sissy, clearly worried, frantically ran ahead of me. She had brought the spotlight from the boat. Evidently, whoever rigged it had made it portable.

It wasn't a moonlit night, as you'd hope to see in a spot named Moon Island. Instead, clouds moved about the sky in bunches, threatening rain. Even if Mrs. Moon just walked into the woods, she wouldn't fair well in a downpour. The spotlight glare opened up sections of scrub, mud, and tree trunks for a few feet, but at the edges, darkness prevailed. Each time Sissy called out "Grandma!," animals darted under bushes or headed for the water. At the lake edge, I stopped and took the light from her. Could the old lady have tried to haul out Grandpa by herself?

The spotlight hit a couple of eyes that darted beneath the surface. Alligators were here, then. Something squealed in terror a few feet away from the shore. When I pointed the light that way, an owl glared back at me from the ground, his talons planted firmly inside a rat.

Away from the lake and the house, the island turned to solid forest, a barrier for the best of hunters and an impossibility for an old lady.

"She won't be in there." I said and shined the light onto thick tree trunks surrounded by high bushes. Some were palmettos that would produce a nasty stab if you leaned against them.

"You don't know Grandma," said Sissy. "She goes where the voices tell her."

"She hears voices?"

"Says she hears Grandpa, doesn't she?"

"So do you."

Sissy didn't answer that one. Somehow, I was going to have to get a doctor to look at Mrs. Moon. I couldn't stop thinking about the possibilities of early Alzheimers or schizophrenia.

In the distance, the high-pitched sound of an old man yelling *whooooeee!* penetrated the night life of the island and sent birds scurrying to the heights. It was followed by another *whooooeee!* of a different pitch. I recognized it as Edwin following Pasquin's lead.

"They've found her!" I said. "Let's head back to the house."

When we reached the old structure, a rugged man who looked like he'd been plucked from the 1960s and aged on the spot, rocked back and forth. He blew smoke into the air and smiled with his eyes closed. The night screams meant nothing to him.

Another, closer, *whooooeee!* came from the tie-ups. Sissy and I ran to meet Pasquin pulling up in his boat. Edwin stood in front, ready to secure it to a pole, his grin showing how pleased he was with their venture.

Grandma Moon sat in the small boat like a stiff-backed lady, her pocketbook in her lap and her gloved hands draped across it. She wore a flowery dress and had tried to attach an artificial rose to her thin hair. A suitcase rested on the floor.

"We found her waiting at the crossing. Tide was in, so she didn't want to walk in the water. Said she was waiting for Aaron to come and get her."

"Aaron?" Sissy frowned. "He's in jail and wouldn't come and get her even if he could."

Pasquin moved out of the boat. While Edwin held it steady, he bent toward Mrs. Moon and offered his hand.

"Madame," he said.

She smiled and offered him a gloved hand, rose from the boat and stepped on shore. It was regal, Southern-bayou style.

Mrs. Moon insisted on taking Pasquin's arm. He shrugged and led her to the house. Sissy followed along, her scowl still on a young face. Edwin stayed with the boat, using the flashlight to detect water snakes.

Patel stood on the front porch, his face grinning in relief. Trukee never acknowledged we were there. Pasquin, all the Cajun gentleman, gently took the woman's hand from his arm and turned it over to Sissy.

"Come on, Grandma," she said and pulled her inside the old door.

"Maybe she needs better watching," I said.

"Corwin says that's Sissy's job when she's out of school. He's not going to like it when he hears she wasn't here." Patel's voice moved rapidly in the staccato English from his native country.

I looked at Pasquin who stepped forward and patted the man on his shoulder. "He won't like it that you let her get away, either. Isn't that really what you're worried about?"

Patel's eyes opened wide.

"But, don't worry, fellow, you needn't tell him. Just make sure Sissy doesn't say anything." He looked toward Trukee. "I don't think this guy even knows what happened."

Patel both shook and nodded his head. Corwin would get no tales out of him.

Sissy stayed with her grandmother. There was no gesture of thanking us or asking us to stay for tea. Southern hospitality had run its course in this house.

"Makes you wonder at how far the old ways of the South have fallen into ruin," I said to Pasquin as he guided the boat back into the waters that would take us home.

"Look," I said and watched Pasquin gently pull the tiller as though it was an appendage growing from his own arm. "When I was growing up, good ol' boys and girls for that matter would swim in anything. I remember swinging from vines into dark bottomed creeks where moccasins basked on logs. I even crawled up on a couple of those logs."

"Me too," said Pasquin, "and sometimes without a stitch of protection on my skin." He chuckled, his vocal rhythm matching that of the gently lapping water.

"You mean naked," I smiled. I had once watched, from a hiding place behind a big oak, boys flying naked off vines.

"Miracle we didn't get covered in leeches." He gazed into the air and let the wind brush his white hair away from his face, his straw hat tossed at his feet.

Edwin giggled at the thought of naked boys flying off vines. At least that's what we thought. Maybe he saw two snakes dancing in the water.

"That's what I'm trying to say here. Sissy doesn't know how to swim. Her father said he never swam in the lake. Yet, the trespassing boys swim there. Even the alligator doesn't keep them away."

"You'd think the Moons would be all over that water," he said.

"Exactly. So why aren't they? Is the spectre of Grandpa in the depths too scary for a superstitious family? Or some other reason?"

Pasquin threw up one hand in a shrug of not knowing and not much caring at the moment.

We putted slowly through the briny water, under the bridge, and finally into clear river water. Edwin, in man-child wonder, watched the flow of the water in the dim boat lights until he dozed off, his snoring scaring water birds from their plant nests.

"Somebody's got to do something about that Grandma situation," said Pasquin. "Bad enough for the elders, but to turn it all over to a little girl just don't seem right." He turned, slapped the hat back on his head, and looked at me from under the brim. "And it's not safe having a little kid—a little girl kid—around that pothead on the front porch."

I nodded. "Pothead? When did you start talking in those terms?"

"You know what I mean." Pasquin was having no joking. He smelled trouble. I did, too, but longed for that little voice that told me to *stay out of it, Luanne.*

Our peaceful river was disrupted when a barking sounded off my landing. It was one of greeting and concern, almost like a worried mother asking "Where have you been?"

"Plato's back," said Pasquin.

Edwin jerked and sat up at the dog's sound, which had turned to an anxious whimpering as he danced about the boards.

"Okay!" I said and scratched his ears when I hit the landing. I turned to wave at Pasquin who wouldn't wait until I went inside since the trusty dog was there to guard me.

"What would you do, old sod," I said to Plato as he lay at my feet after a hefty bowl of stinky canned food. "Would you rescue the girl?" He looked up at me from his headrest on the floor, his tail flopping back and forth. He was swamp dog without equal. I often felt like following him to see what he did out in those woods all day. "Of course, you would." I rested my head on the recliner.

I awoke in the recliner when the sun came through the window. Plato, still on the floor, had dragged his pillow near my feet as though making sure I wouldn't go out again. His tail thumped against the stuffing, sending bits of dust into the sunlight.

My back and legs didn't want to move. "I'm getting too old to sleep in a chair," I said to Plato, who followed me to the kitchen.

My first thought had been to talk the whole situation over with Vernon, my lover and companion and fellow diver, but I didn't want to place him in a position of having to follow the rules. He was a deputy after all, and we were talking about child welfare here. He'd get the hint if I did anything anyway. I decided it might be best to talk to Sissy's aunt or cousin, or whatever the relation she had with the woman.

My head swam right along with the currents as I rehearsed what I might say to Sissy's teacher when I showed up at her door. If she wasn't in the book, and I couldn't con the information out of someone on Moon Island, I would have to ask Vernon to find it for me.

The phone book came through with the goods. There she was: R. Moon, teacher, grades 1-7, listed in the business section. The address was inside Fogarty Spring, the little town named after my own ancestors. "No wonder Sissy knew the way down that river. She probably navigates it every day during the school week."

CHAPTER FIVE

Mama's Table served up the best and biggest of its Southern fried fish and seafood for Sunday dinner—lunch to the rest of the world. The stack of lightly battered and freshly shucked oysters, surrounded by homemade hushpuppies, and freshly grated slaw could not, for anyone's money, be called lunch. To Southerners, at least the older ones, lunch was something between two pieces of bread and a bowl of peaches for a side dish.

I figured Rachel Moon would be someone who went to church. I decided to eat from Mama's Table and chat with the locals while I waited for her to return. Mama, herself, would be a source of local lore about the Moons, especially if Rachel Moon had lived in Fogarty Spring for very long.

Inside the waterside cafe, I searched for law enforcement, planning to avoid any deputy hearing my inquiries about the Moons. Weary eyed crime scene people or deputies were absent from the tables so the swamp must have been tame last night.

"Where's that old man?" asked Mama. She still walked with a limp from a knee replacement she'd had the year before. Pasquin said it was from habit and not pain. The other knee had to be done one day, but when Mama turned the cafe over to a friend temporarily, it was near disaster and reputation ruining. In the end, she closed down the place until she could stand long enough to fry fish.

"Pasquin? Probably sleeping off a long night of bourbon. Edwin may have stayed at his place, and you know how they can put away that stuff." I pointed to the big platter. I didn't need all that food, but I'd take some home to Plato.

"That old man will kill his liver," she said and laughed at her own words. "Hell, he probably don't even have one anymore."

"Edwin would be the one to suffer," I said. "I don't think he drinks when he's not around Pasquin, except for beer."

"Look, Luanne, honey, you can bet old Pasquin didn't sit up hours drinking with that mud-for-brains Edwin as his only company. Likely he called in some of his river friends."

"Speaking of friends, I need to ask you about somebody who lives here in Fogarty Springs."

Mama smiled, her round red face squinting. A new perm flared over her head. "I figured you came here to eat alone for a reason. You normally would have that Vernon charmer with you. What's the matter? Couldn't get him to spend the night?"

"Oh, Mama," I said and winked, "he has his own place. He never spends the night."

"I'll be back with your food and you can put me under the third degree, but don't give me none of that Miss Prude stuff." She turned and shuffled her thighs to the kitchen. Eating her own food was her number one indulgence.

Mama's waitress help came in soon after she took my order. She had a couple of assistant cooks in the kitchen, but she wasn't going to want to sit still for long.

She squeezed her chubby legs and tight white uniform into the seat across from me. She had placed the oval platter of shrimp, oysters, grouper, and hushpuppies in front of me, and put the separate bowl of slaw on the side. Without asking, she sat down a half gallon of iced tea.

"You didn't ask, but I know you want these." She added another bowl of cheese grits next to the slaw. Fish just would not do without grits on the side. "And I got a little for myself." She pulled out a spoon and began scooping some freshly made banana pudding into her mouth. "Now what you got to say?"

"Rachel Moon?"

She looked up at me with the spoon still in her mouth. "Rachel Moon? That old bitty who lives down the river road?"

"Is that where she lives?"

"Just walk out of here and go about six houses straight ahead on the dirt road. She lives in an old white frame kind of set back in some oaks. What would you want with that old thing?"

"She can't be all that old. I figured about sixtyish."

"Not by age, but she's in another era. Still balls up her gray hair in the back. Still teaches kids even though she retired from the county system. Tidy with little doilies all over the furniture."

"Sounds like you've been inside."

"A few times. She used to have a cooking club that met there and asked me in a few times to demonstrate biscuit making to a few young women."

I popped seafood into my mouth, trying to savor it slowly but really wolfing it down. It was habit forming, and being fresh, not at all hard to take. Mama scraped the bottom of her banana pudding bowl and shoved it to the end of the table. The waitress came by and took it away.

"Have you ever seen her little kids that she home schools?"

"I heard about them, but she keeps them down on her end of the road. I think she may be afraid to let them get too close to the water, or maybe it's the fishermen who come in here sometimes.

Her neighbors say that when she goes out in the yard with them, she gathers them about her like a hen with chicks."

"There's one girl, Sissy Moon, her cousin, who comes daily in her own boat. Do you see her tie up?"

"No, and I wouldn't. Rachel has her own tie up right behind her house. Probably wouldn't let a little girl tie up here with all these men anyway." Mama laughed. She'd been around such ruggedness for over thirty years and lived to feed them some more.

"How many kids does she teach?"

Mama shrugged, her plump shoulders threatening to rip the sleeves on the uniform. "Like I said, she keeps them down there. I don't think there are many. I'd see them once in a while if she had ten or twelve. That little house couldn't hold a bunch."

"And if I pay her a visit?" I didn't want some scared old lady standing on a porch with a shotgun.

"She's as cordial as a Southern lady gets, Luanne. Now, if you were Pasquin—or worse, Edwin—she might run you off her yard."

"When's church over?"

I had about thirty minutes to kill before Rachel had her soul filled with Southern righteousness and would head home to fill her belly with Southern cooking. I had just returned from washing the shrimp batter from my fingers when I saw people at the door of the little cafe, wearing pretty dresses and suits which reminded me of my childhood. They came in social groups, back slapping and talking about the latest hunting trip. About to partake in gluttony, they lost no time in speaking of killing. The Ten Commandments didn't last all that long after the doxology was sung.

Avoiding most of the crowd, I sneaked out the door and headed straight down the road toward the house where Rachel lived. This town was named after an ancestor of mine. Did I live up to his example? Back then, getting shrimp and moonshine up this river to market must have required some illegal shenanigans.

I stood before a gingerbread cracker house—meaning a white wood frame with a covered porch and lacy woodwork attached to the edges and around the windows. Most likely, the porch would be enclosed in Cape Cod but here you could walk right up and sit in a rocker, even watch the owner come walking down the road.

Miss Rachel Moon's dress was too tight, not because she was some brazen woman but because she'd had too many helpings of grits and hush puppies at the last fish fry. She carried a white purse on her arm, Queen Elizabeth-style, and wore little girl pumps with low heels as she maneuvered the cracked and dusty sidewalks.

"Oh, dear!" she said and held up her Bible like it might ward off strangers. "I didn't see you sitting there."

"I'm Luanne Fogarty, Miss Moon. I need to speak to you about one of your pupils."

Miss Moon seemed not to be afraid of me, but like Mama said, she might not allow a man inside her neat house. It took three locks to undo before the door opened into a tidy dark living room.

"Please sit and sip some tea while I change out of this awful dress." She tugged at the hips while setting the filled glass on a coaster. "I just can't get used to wearing slacks to church. All the other ladies do, even some older than I am. I was just always taught…" She drifted away from me, down a hall, and I supposed into her bedroom.

Miss Moon seemed to want her place to give a homey impression. Instead, it gave me the creeps. The sofa, chair, and love seat patterns matched with sunny yellow flowers surrounded by dark blue, almost black, foliage. A few photos in frames lined the mantel over a fireplace covered with a Victorian screen. The window curtains, some dark hue of green, closed off any light.

"I keep them closed so the sun won't fade the upholstery," she said when she returned, attired now in comfortable slacks and a pullover shirt. "Would you like a bit of light in here?" She turned and opened the curtains without waiting for my answer. Behind the dark colored drapes were gauzy panels of white. They let in light but kept out the view.

"Have I interrupted your lunch time?" I asked, realizing I'd filled my gut with Mama's Table delicacies while Rachel prayed.

"Oh, don't worry about me. I need to take off pounds. I've got a cold salad waiting in the fridge." She sat in a chair, folded her hands in her lap, and smiled at me. The face had lined a bit, but with some makeup and a bottle of hair color, she'd be a pretty woman.

"Sissy Moon is your cousin, I understand?" I took another sip of the tea. When the condensation on the glass began to drip, Miss Moon grabbed a tissue and tapped the droplets from the coffee table.

"Sissy, yes," she wrinkled her forehead and looked away for a moment. "Poor kid. She has no business living out there with those strange folks."

"Her father?"

"Strangest of all," she frowned and shook her head. "He's got full custody now. At least I get her here during the school year."

"He didn't have custody before?"

"Oh, yes. Since her mother took off, and that was some time ago. Poor dear. Living there is just so hard." Her voice came down on the last two words, like someone had thrust a fist in her gut.

I tried to continue, but Rachel Moon stood up, went into the kitchen and brought back her own glass of tea.

"Before I go on, just what is your interest in Sissy?"

I began to tell her who I was and that I'd been called there by Sissy's great-grandmother. When I tried to explain the work I did for the sheriff, she stopped me.

"Yes, I know who you are. Otherwise, I'd never have let you in here. What I want to know is why you need to come to me about her."

"She is convinced old Mrs. Moon is hearing her dead husband. I don't buy that. Although she may be hearing something. Sissy seems to hear it, too. We did a brief dive search of the lake and found nothing, but Mrs. Moon says her husband walked in and never came out." I sipped the last of the tea, mostly melted ice by now.

Rachel pushed her aging body deep into the chair and gripped the glass with both hands. "I dislike that lake," she said. "I hated it as a child and don't taken to it now."

"Could you say that again?"

"What?"

"I'm sorry, but you said 'don't taken to it,' a phrase quite like Sissy and her family use."

Miss Moon blushed and made a "shoo-away" sign with her hand. "I'm sorry. I was an English teacher, after all. It's just the words the family used. When I was around them, I talked like them." She shrugged.

"Don't be embarrassed," I said. "It would seem you've got your own dialect going out there on that island."

"It wasn't only the island family. The rest of us didn't live far away from the river. It's just the way we talked to each other." She leaned over and stared at me. "Please don't think I speak that way in the classes I run."

I smiled and bet silently that Rachel Moon slipped into dialect every time the kids gave her a headache.

"Tell me about the island." I leaned back in the tidy sofa.

"I never lived there," she said. "I lived with my parents closer to Carabelle. They liked to work a fish camp in the summer and sent me to visit Moon Island almost every year." She stared into space for a moment, a slight smile on her face. "It was a magical place for a while. You know how kids are. Big old house with lots of rooms and porches, boats stopping by all the time. We went swimming on one side of that old lake, had such fun. I never could swing from a vine, but the boys did. Made huge splashes and pretended to fall on alligators. Beatrice Moon—that's the lady you met—made the best hard-icing chocolate cake you can eat. She had one of these built-in corner hutches and always kept a cake in there. Sometimes it was white coconut, sometimes a caramel with pecans all over the top, but it was the hard-icing chocolate that was the best treat." She stopped talking, stared at the floor and smiled for several moments.

"Then you knew the family members, the three children from Mrs. Moon and her grandsons, Corwin and Aaron?"

"Yes. We were playmates to some extent. I was closest to Margie, old Mrs. Moon's second daughter. She was just a few years older than Corwin, her nephew." She looked up suddenly. "I'm not really all that close in blood kin. My daddy was a second cousin to old Mr. Moon."

"The one who jumped into the lake?"

She stared at me for a second, frowning and seeming to be in deep thought. "Yes," she said slowly, "that one."

"I know how it is with Southern families," I said. "It doesn't matter if you're second, third, fourth cousins in distance. You're still family and will visit."

She relaxed and smiled. "And I did visit that place."

She said no more, but got into another staring gaze.

"Sissy? How did she come to be a student of yours?"

Miss Moon nearly dropped her glass when she came out of her reverie. "Oh, I suggested that. You see, she was going to a public school that required a boat ride to a landing, then a walk to a school bus stop, then a long ride to a nasty little school where the test scores are rock bottom. Half the time, she didn't even go because Corwin or one of the boarders was too busy to take her to the bus. She was too little to pilot herself then.

"I'd been wanting to do something with my time since I retired and when I heard about home schooling, I applied."

"Was that difficult?"

"Not at all. I still had a state teacher's credential, a room where I could set up class, and I drew up the required plans. I even get a teacher's discount on texts if I need them."

"May I see the spot where you teach?"

She grinned now and stood to lead me to a room at the end of the hallway. It had once been a sun porch, a prized room for people who live in humid territory. It had walls halfway up and windows the rest of the way.

"I have this long table which serves as a desk, good chairs, bookcases, chalk board, a television set, and some maps on this pole." Rachel moved about the neat room, pointing to a layout that had been planned and kept in perfect order.

"You've got all the textbooks," I said as I leaned over a bookcase. They weren't purchased on her discount, but were stamped with the name of a public school district. Most likely outdated books she got free. The maps were on library poles, probably more rejects from a public library. I didn't check to see if the Russian one was still the USSR. It wouldn't matter. Miss Moon would set them straight.

"I've got exactly what the girls need," she said.

"Girls?"

"Oh, yes. I don't bother with boys. Too rowdy. I've got three girls now. The fourth one moved to Texas with her family."

"And what kind of student is Sissy?"

"Oh, Sissy," she did her moaning thing again. "I started all this for her. She's such a little independent cuss." She giggled. "Sorry, but sometimes she's a handful."

"Smart, I'd guess."

"Very smart, but sometimes a smart aleck. I wanted her to live here. I have so much room. She'd have local kids to meet, and she'd get away from that situation on the island."

"I take it she didn't want to live here?"

"She wants to take care of that old lady. She said if she could come, too, she'd live here. But," she glared at me and pointed her finger, "I had enough of that crazy woman when I grew up. I do not want her living in my house." The hard-icing chocolate cake didn't seem to make much difference.

"Miss Moon," I hesitated, not knowing if this woman would toss me out the door or go deeper into family secrets, "who would take care of the old lady if Sissy moved away?"

Rachel sat up straight as though she'd do a self-righteous *harrumpf,* but she shook her head and closed her eyes.

"Most likely that awful Corwin. He might try and put her in a home—a charity one, mind you. He's not going to spend any money on her. Now," she leaned toward me, the finger pointing again, "don't get me wrong. There's money somewhere, I'm sure. They just live like they're dirt-poor trash. Well, trash they are, but the dirt-poor is debatable."

"What was it like to visit them in the summers?" I was sure fact and feeling were mixing here.

"Fun, at first." Rachel seemed to sag, her defiant attitude changing to passivity. "At the very first, I guess, it was all running and swimming and finding things in the woods out there. Like kids are bound to do."

"What changed?"

Rachel sighed. "I'm not sure what caused it, but the boys got rough, the girls became unhappy and cried a lot, and that ghastly old man!"

"Mr. Moon?"

"Yes, he was just a tyrant. Tried to bully us. Kept bellowing at his wife. She'd screech back." She chuckled to herself. "Ever hear the term fishwife? Well, that's Mrs. Moon. She smoked for years, not something ladies were supposed to do. It caused that shrill voice to turn octaves lower. She sounds more like a loud foghorn today."

"Were you around when Mr. Moon went into the lake?"

"That old thing? He swam in that lake every day of his life far as I know. Or, every day he was around his home."

"No, I mean when he went in and drowned, or so it seems."

Rachel frowned and stared at me. "I wouldn't know about that." She stood up. "I'll get more tea."

It wasn't really an offer, but a gesture to say our conversation was done. I declined the tea and said I needed to get going.

"Could I come back sometime and see how you teach at home?"

She stared at me again.

"I'm a teacher, too, you know. I study dialects sometimes." It was pretty much a lie. I hadn't worked on a dialect since I did my dissertation.

"Yes, but call first, please. We sometimes go out for nature studies and other field trips." She put the tea pitcher back on the tray and hurried to the door to hold it for me.

CHAPTER SIX

My visit with Rachel Moon clouded rather than clarified the situation. Like most closed circle families who live in remote places, they had their secrets. Painful as they may be, sharing them with others was more so.

It was nearly dark when Pasquin rapped at my screen door. Plato stood beside him, hassling and wagging his tail.

"Old dog met me on the path," said Pasquin. He used the torn edge of his straw hat to stroke the dog's back. Plato shook as though it tickled him.

"Some guard dog, you are," I said and let them both onto the porch. That's where Pasquin stayed. He didn't care much for air conditioning, especially at night. The humid air suited him.

"Just rest in a rocker. I'll get some lemonade."

"Poor a little rum in it, Luanne." Pasquin chuckled and yanked on Plato's tail. The dog pretended to bite him.

"Sorry, old man. I don't keep any around the house."

It wasn't a rule that Pasquin needed liquor in his drinks, but he had late nights at his house, entertaining swamp folk, his old cadre of friends, and some younger ones he'd met over the years. Even after a lifetime of knowing him, I hadn't met all of them.

I passed him a tall glass of cold lemonade and tossed a bought doggie treat to Plato. He'd much prefer a thick ham bone, but I didn't have any.

Pasquin rocked, setting a slow, steady rhythm with the wooden rockers on the wooden floor. I knew it was a winding up to tell me something. I sat down next to him in the other rocker. We both stared into the fading sunset and waited for the moss draped trees to turn completely black.

"You remember Gavi, the man who lives out near Portu Landing?"

"Yes, the fellow with no teeth. The one who helped us with the bilge case."

"Living out past the briny water, he knows a lot about the island folk. I figured maybe he'd get a word in about the Moon family legend. He'll be shucking oysters tomorrow, in case you'd like to talk to him."

"Morning or evening?" I had classes to teach the next day. The university frowned on canceling for work on a case, even when they used me for a bit of favorable press.

"Morning. Gavi don't hold up too well after lunch." Pasquin chuckled.

"Too old or too much grog?"

"Hadn't heard that word "grog" in quite a spell, ma'am." Pasquin wasn't going to answer, but if he did, it would most likely be a bit of both. Gavi had to be his age, eighty-plus, and sipping his grog was in his tradition of Portuguese descendants on these waters.

"Will he be shucking the next morning?" I didn't have a morning class scheduled but would have to be back in time for a one o'clock.

We made the arrangements. Pasquin would gas up his boat and haul us both from the river to the briny water and into the

Gulf for a bumpy ride into Apalachicola Bay. Oyster boats brought in their loads, and the shucking houses hired men like Gavi to do quick shucks for wholesale. Others would pack them in the shell for oyster bars where customers slid the uncooked creatures laced with hot sauce down their throats.

"Pasquin, did you know Miss Rachel Moon, a school teacher?"

"Rachel Moon. She taught in the county elementary, I believe. Known for a healthy bit of morality mixed in with the 'rithmetic."

"And she has lived in Fogarty Spring for a long time."

Pasquin nodded and sipped the lemonade. He stared, or at least gazed with glazed eyes, at the night in front of him. He rocked slowly and came to a stop.

We both heard the silence which was as startling as a scream in the night. Not an owl or a cricket, not even a frog chorus. The forest had gone dark and, like an abandoned stage, the actors weren t saying a thing.

"Something's out there," I whispered.

Pasquin only nodded. He looked down at Plato whose fur began to rise. He hadn't barked or growled. Instead of doing his usual "get off my territory" thing, he let the hair drop and padded to the screen door where he sat on his haunches. Soon, the tail moved slowly back and forth across the dusty boards.

"Must be a friend," I said and stood up. No sound at all came from the landing. Not even a night bird flew from the bushes around the house.

"Something white coming down the path," said Pasquin as he raised himself half out of his rocking chair. "Something small, and I'll be damned! Girlie!"

"Sissy?"

"I stopped because my motor gave out way back there," the little girl said and pointed back toward Fogarty Spring. "I had to use the paddles. Your dock was closest."

"Good heavens! Sissy, you must stop roaming around on the river after dark."

I opened the door and helped her up the steps. Plato gave her a sniff and a lick, wagging his tail in greeting. She sat down on a footstool and scratched his ears.

"What are you doing out this time of night?" asked Pasquin.

"I had to get Grandma's medicine." She pulled a small plastic bag with a drug store logo on it from her pocket.

"Why doesn't Corwin do this?"

"He's on a job. Said he might be gone for a few days. When he didn't come back, and Trukee and Patel went on jobs, too, I had to take care of it." She smiled and her thin face and straggly hair took on a healthier glow, for a moment.

"She needs the medicine bad?" asked Pasquin.

"She was out." Sissy passed the bag to Pasquin who took the bottle out and squinted in the dim porch light.

"Sleeping tablets," he said. "She's got a sleeping problem. Not too rare in people her age." He looked down at Sissy. "If she's taking this stuff, she's got to have a regular doctor."

Sissy nodded. "I take her in the boat every three months to the walk-in clinic."

"In Palmetto Springs?"

She shook her head. "Nope. The little one in Fogarty Spring. Rachel meets us at the dock. She takes us there."

I looked at Pasquin. "The same place Edwin visits now and then."

"I suppose Rachel takes you to eat at Mama's Table when you're there?" Pasquin shot a glance my way.

"Oh no. Rachel don't taken to that place. She says there's too many drunkard fishermen about for her to enjoy the meal. She cooks something herself."

"And your grandmother gives you no trouble on these trips?" I didn't think I'd want to be mid-river in a fragile boat with that old lady.

"Only when I make her wear her life jacket." Sissy smiled. "She likes the trip, and she likes Rachel a lot."

I was puzzled. Rachel had said she'd had enough of Mrs. Moon as a child, yet Mrs. Moon liked her. The doctor's visits hadn't been part of our conversation.

"Well," said Pasquin, "I guess I'll have to get my boat and tow yours back to the dock in Fogarty Springs for repair."

"No!" Sissy was on her feet. "Can you tow me to Moon Island? I'll get someone to fix it there. We can't afford no repairman at Fogarty."

I looked at Pasquin. "Another ride on the water at night."

And the night was long. Pasquin had walked to my house and had to walk back to get his boat and a tow rope. Once he had attached the two boats, the three of us and Plato climbed into his and began the long trek on water to Moon Island. Sissy's boat followed Pasquin's, staying in the wake.

"Watch for a big boat," she said. "There's some deliveries made at night." She hunched in the bottom of the boat, and when Plato got tired of the breeze in his face, he hopped down with her. By the time we reached the island, she was sound asleep, her hand draped loosely around the dog's neck.

"Better get up, Sissy," I said and shook her gently. Plato stood and licked her face. "We're here."

Sissy's face looked old in the boat light. She was too young to be so tired, I thought.

"You've got the medicine?" asked Pasquin.

Without a word, Sissy checked her pocket for the bag and bottle, nodded, and held onto the side of the boat as we lifted her to the shore. One foot slipped in the mud on shore, and she scraped it on the grass as she moved up the hill.

"I guess we'll tie up her boat here and someone will find it in the morning," said Pasquin.

I held the boat steady while he untied the tow rope and fastened it to a post in the water.

"I don't like this, Pasquin. I'm going to follow her until she gets inside." I didn't wait for him to protest, but climbed onto the bank and followed the path to the big house.

The place was dark, not even a porch light left on for a little girl who would surely not come home before dark. I wondered if she just disappeared one night would Mrs. Moon say she walked into the lake and never came up again. The porch was half-lit by the moon and a few stars, when they weren't covered by clouds. I caught sight of the chair where Trukee sat and smoked. Sissy nearly crawled up the old steps, leaning over to balance herself. She let the front door slam behind her, and I saw a light go on in the living room. How safe she was, I didn't know, but at least she was out of the elements.

On my way back, I heard some breathy movements in the distance. Was that supposed to be Mr. Moon's ghost? Sounded more like a dredging machine to me.

My world the next day could have been thousands of miles from the crumbling Moon house on Moon Island. The brick walls of the linguistics building had stood there since the place had been founded. It smelled old and chalky in the solid dark halls, and the classroom doors stood open to aging desks. Students were dragging in for eight o'clock classes and didn't like it a bit. They had stopped at the coffee kiosk outside and hauled their books in backpacks and carried lattes in cardboard holders. I often wondered if I were lecturing to humans or cups in these early classes.

"I saw you coming in," said Manny, the department chair, whose hair got longer and thinner each year he was farther away from the 1960s. "Got you a coffee." He passed a cup to me. "Tastes better than that stuff we make."

"Thanks," I said and took the tall cup even though I'd had two strong home brews before I left my end of the swamp. "You got a minute?"

"Do you?" he said. "I thought you had an early class."

"Just a question that may reach back into your memory cells."

"That could take hours." He tapped his head. "These cells move pretty slow in this old computer these days."

I nodded and smiled. I agreed with that. He had dwindled to the position of department historian more than chair. His secretary and assistant took care of most of the scheduling. Any topic for research was pretty much guaranteed approval.

"Has anyone ever done research on old families out near the bay? The oyster and shrimp families and maybe some isolated groups on islands out that way?"

He held the door for me and followed me into my cluttered office of glass and wood partitions. We couldn't hear much through them but we sure could see who was sitting there. I nodded to my colleague who frantically marked grades in a book. It was clear she was near retirement because she didn't enter them directly into her computer.

"Why do you ask? You thinking of doing a paper?" Manny took the only empty chair and sipped on his coffee. "I never could drink the hot stuff through these special lids," he said and pulled it off to let it steam.

"Well," I stopped. It wouldn't be right to say it's all for a case I may or may not be working on, or that it originated with the sheriff's department. It wasn't connected now, anyway. "I've come across some interesting people and wondered if anyone had done the same."

Manny leaned back in the chair and held the coffee cup close to his chest with both hands. He closed his eyes and resembled an old man in meditation.

"I can't think of anyone we've got here now, but do you remember that former professor, a woman, who visited us a few years back? She was a kind of pioneer in the field. Did lots of local dialects." He opened his eyes and shook his head. "Can't think of her name but she's got emeritus after it. Funny old dame."

"Funny old dame? I'll look her up," I said. I realized he was talking about Professor Iris Henderson, a grand old lady who never married but paddled about the rivers in her canoe with her recorder and wrote article after article on dialects. She hadn't come around the university in several years and I had no idea if she still had her mental abilities.

The class this morning was one in phonetics, a subject all majors had to take as prerequisite to more advanced courses. One subject was the glottal stop, and a student who had grown up in London started on a string of the sounds prevalent in Cockney. He thought it terribly funny. Having found all the glottal stops, he changed to the "h" dropping and laughter began among a group of immature eighteen-year-olds. In the best of my calm voices, I stopped them to remind them that a linguist does not judge and poke fun. He merely listens and documents.

I spent my lunch time in the old records part of the linguistic administration office—a fancy name for Manny's private bedlam. His own works, and honors gained for work, among South American Indians, were jammed into a rickety bookcase on one side of a dusty window. Photos, yellowed now, sat on the top shelf. They showed a young man with the same hair style—and lots more of it—in jeans, a dirty tee-shirt, and sandals. Most of us swore he still wore those sandals. He had joined a tribe who wore almost nothing and decorated their ears and noses. The bare-breasted women stood in a group, smiling and staring at the young Manny. These were the people who talked to him, who let him record their voices over and over again, whose language he learned and still spoke when he thought about it. All the books on the shelves beneath the photo were about this language, using the linguistic jargon of schwas and glottal stops. He loved these natives, revered them for being able to make all those sounds no English speaker ever could. But, then, Manny never taught a beginning course. His graduate students had learned respect.

"Just look in the bottom file," his secretary said. She was nearly his age, but her dress had changed with the times. "It should be under Retired Faculty."

I rummaged through the old files and came up with Professor Henderson's address and phone number, or at least the last one we had on record for her.

CHAPTER SEVEN

Iris Henderson lived where she had always lived. In a library, she served tea using a silver service and we sat next to a shelving-unit that I was afraid would topple over on us from the weight of books.

"I didn't acquire all these books by myself," she said as she set the tray and service on a central table that was antique enough to draw huge sums at auction. "I inherited them from a grandfather and a father." She poured an aromatic brew into a fragile cup that must have come down from her grandmother. "Poor dears. They ran out of males when I came along. I had to be the one they educated." She laughed, her gray hair coming loose from the combs. "They had no idea what I was doing when I ran all over the woods with a recorder. Of course, in the very early days, I tried to bring the informants into the office where I could use the old reel to reel recorder. Best thing ever when they came out with the portable cassettes."

Iris was delighted when I called her to ask about some dialect studies she'd done. She insisted I have tea with her after my last class and invited me to her two story house in a wooded patch of land next to a new suburb of million dollar homes. She had built the place herself—or at least designed it. The outside was solid wood with angles that resembled a puzzle game. Inside, the rooms were few but large. She had built just what she wanted—a private and convenient house for one single lady. It occupied a corner lot where two secondary roads met, both leading to Tallahassee.

"I miss the linguistics stuff, you know. Find myself sitting still and eavesdropping on conversations just to pick up accents. You won't believe how this city has changed. Lots of French and Irish here now, English, too, and East Indians."

"Are you like Henry Higgins, able to identify origins?" I took a bite of some exotic pastry filled with cream and blueberries.

"Oh, my, I guess I am. But, I'm always open to finding something new."

"You did several studies a few years back on shrimp fishermen and their families."

"Yes, interesting time that was. They tend to be a close group, not used to university people. I had to visit among them a while to gain their trust or they wouldn't let me record them." Iris wiped her long fingers on a cloth napkin and scraped back her chair. "Here, I've got something about that." She kicked a stool and stood atop it, her bare old lady legs keeping steady. She wore a denim skirt and running shoes with no socks.

"Is there anything about the people who live on Moon Island, or is that a place you never covered?"

Iris stopped in her tracks just as she got down from the stool. "Moon Island? Oh! I wanted on that place but never got the chance. Is this what we're talking about?"

"Exactly. I've got reasons for asking that may not be totally linguistic, but we can start there."

"I love this!" She tossed the book onto the stool and rejoined me at the table. "I've heard about you and your police antics. Are we talking about that?"

"Maybe, but I'd prefer you not mention it yet, not even to the police—or the sheriff."

"Never! Now, what can I help you with?" She held up a hand. "Wait. I'll help only if you promise to get me on that island. I'm good with boats and pretty agile, in an old lady sort of way."

I smiled. "I'll do my best. I might even let you listen to my old friend, a kind of north Florida Cajun, who has lived on the river his entire life."

"Yes!" she let the "s" hiss a bit.

"The Moon family that I've met so far, including a preteen girl, use a peculiar form of past tense. They use the past participle of some verbs and stick an "ed" on it rather than use the past form. I hear "takened" a lot for "took." And, they'll use "take" to describe actions, something like "he takened to eating early."

"Isolated dialect. I've seen patterns similar to this, but I'd like to give this field one last hurrah from me and write an article on Moon Island. When can we go?"

How did I get from asking a professor emeritus about work she'd done to taking her to Moon Island? Iris Henderson was not done with life yet.

"Maybe we better start with Pasquin, the Cajun. Moon Island has to be handled with a bit of delicacy."

"I may not look it, honey, but I can be delicate. I've got gray hair, wrinkles and sagging flesh to make me look as delicate—or say fragile—as you want."

We spent the time after the tea roaming around Iris' house. She had two huge bedrooms, each with its own bath, upstairs, and the library, kitchen, living and dining rooms downstairs with closets everywhere, their woodsy doors blending in with the wood on the walls. In spite of her tall, narrow windows, the house was dark because of the heavy oak growth outside. She had no grass, only a forest floor where pine needles and leaves shed from various tree varieties. A bird bath sat among the oaks, its once white sides covered in green algae.

"I still clean out the bowl and fill it with water. Love to watch the birds flap about in it."

Hummingbird feeders hung from three different low-slung branches, their red-colored liquid attracting the long-billed hoverers.

"You won't find any squirrel traps on my land," she said. "I like the little imps, smart as tacks. In the years when the oaks put out lots of acorns, they have a chattering festival out here." She opened the door to a shed the size of a two-car garage. "My boats," she said. A long blue canoe with an iris flower painted on the side hung on a wall rack. On the other wall, a kayak.

"I try to do the river trips with the groups to keep up my abilities, but don't always get to meet their schedules. I prefer the canoe. Gives me more freedom than the kayak, and it's what got me about in my dialect collecting days. And I used to have a motor boat, but keeping up the engine is troublesome. I sold it to a student."

The shed smelled of humid air and dirt, but there were no spider webs. Iris obviously kept it clean for her boats.

"Good," I said. "We probably won't need these, but it's good to know you can handle a boat."

We walked through the leafy debris back to the main house. Inside, Iris insisted on heating up the tea. She half-way apologized for not serving iced tea, Southern-style. "The Brits," she said, "have it right about hot tea in the afternoon. Peps up the soul." I hadn't heard it put that way, but I guess soul would be a quality of British tea.

"You know, I seem to recall something about the Moon family. Maybe that's why I never got to that place." She frowned and looked up at the tall ceiling. "I can't remember what it was."

"Maybe a disappearing old man?"

"No, I don't remember anything like that."

"It may have been too long ago, 1959 according to legend."

"Too far back. Linguistics was in its infancy then." She poured hot water over new tea bags. "Let it steep a minute or two." She placed the pot on an iron trivet and returned to her bookcases. This time, she reached for some notebooks. "I kept all my notes over the years. Never thought they'd reveal a thing."

Rifling through the pages of one, she gave a frustrated sigh and stuck it back on the shelf and grabbed the one before it. This continued until she found something.

"Here! Yes, this is when I was doing some areas around the St. Marks River, Ochlockonee Bay and around to Carabelle. I ended up in Apalachicola. That's where I found the fishing families and did the book on them." She ran a finger along the handwritten pages. "Moon! Couldn't get on the island because the family said no. Said they had an emergency and couldn't deal with anything else at the moment. December, 1985. This would have been one of the last official studies I did. Now what do you think that emergency was?"

"You didn't check?"

She sat down and smiled at me. "My dear, I was a linguist, looking for speech patterns. I was not a cop looking for clues. That's your realm."

Somehow, I felt Iris was going to like doing the cop side of things, that finding out why something happened even without dialect in mind would interest her. I decided to test the waters.

"Dr. Henderson," I sounded as serious as I could. "Do you think you could try and find out what that emergency was? It might help with a lot of things, and if you want me to get you on the island…"

"Oh, all right," she said. "I guess it's tit for tat. Won't be hard. I'm good at looking into old records. And," she touched my hand, "you must call me Iris. Dr. Henderson ended ages ago."

"I'm Luanne," I said. "In our little jaunts, let's not use Dr. Fogarty."

I left Iris Henderson's dark wood house with the feeling I'd met an ally in mischievousness. All her years hadn't taken away her energy. I was betting that when a lizard dashed into her house, she plucked him from the wall with her own hands and tossed him outside without a flinch.

Vernon was sitting in a rocker on my porch when I pulled up to the carport. Pasquin sat beside him, the two of them keeping a rhythm of clacks on the board.

"You've been busy," said Vernon grinning. "Planning on adopting a little girl?"

I turned to Pasquin whose eyes were closed. He fanned himself with his hat and smiled in the way people who are thinking good thoughts do.

"Okay, old man, what have you been discussing here?"

"Just talking about little girl antics."

"I suppose you mean Sissy Moon?"

"The kid seems pretty resourceful," said Vernon, his grin turning toward the frown stage. "She tends to be out on her own a lot."

"Look, Vernon," I never called him that directly unless a protest was coming down the tracks, "we've never let her go down that river by herself. We always took her home—escorted her there."

"But she is out at night, chugging down a swift current river in a rickety boat. It might not be your idea that she do that, but you haven't reported it, have you?"

"Oh, now we're being the by-the-book lawman. I need to report this kid who goes up and down the river to an agency who will investigate sometime next year, then give a notice to her father that she can't do that." I stared at him.

"Listen, Luanne, I'm not the one complaining here." Vernon moved forward in his chair, leaned over and planted his elbows on his knees, a friendly stance that I'd seen him use a lot when questioning suspects. It was nonthreatening to them. Knowing the reason for it, I felt threatened.

"Okay, then who is complaining?"

"It seems like the kid told her aunt how she'd been by to see you. Even said she admired you. The aunt got concerned about her safety and reported it to a deputy who stopped in to eat at Mama's Table."

"She doesn't eat at Mama's Table. Doesn't like all those evil men who patronize the place."

"The deputy said she caught him at his car."

"And the deputy went to you?"

"He didn't go to Tony," Vernon smiled.

"Well, thank him for that." I walked away from the porch and leaned against an oak tree trunk. When I walked back, I said, "Okay, I'll tell her she shouldn't run that boat alone on the river. Will that take care of things?"

Vernon sighed and smiled, "For now, I suppose. But, one day, child services may have to go out to that island."

It wasn't surprising. The idea of such a child taking care of her great-grandmother while her father was gone most of the time, not to mention living there with boarders, didn't sound ideal. I didn't ask if he knew about the drugs she carried from the Fogarty Spring pharmacy, but it angered me a bit to know the woman had reported her niece but not the prescription medicine.

"Look, I'd like to stay," Vernon looked at me and winked, a gesture not missed by Pasquin, "but I've got a diving job in a sinkhole. Seems some kids knew they were getting caught with weed in the car so they pushed the entire supply into the sink. Only thing is they were too stupid to open the package first."

"Before you go," I said, "do you know what it is that boats deliver at night on this river?"

Vernon looked at me and shrugged. "They're restaurants up and down the banks, and there's a dock past Fogarty Spring where trucks pull in. I've never done any work there, but it's probably fish, shrimp, stuff like that. Why?"

"On one of our escort sessions, we met a fairly large boat that Sissy called a night delivery. I guess I didn't know they did that at night, or at least not much of it. I've lived most of my life on this river, and I didn't know that."

"Wasn't much of it in the recent past," said Pasquin, who had relaxed into a slow rock, still fanning his face. "Did a whole lot of it back in my day. Those old piers at Crawfish Dock just got some new boards. Most likely deliveries are made at high tide. Too shallow for the big boats up at that end during low tide."

Vernon and I stared at Pasquin whose eyes were still closed.

"There's your answer," Vernon said and grinned at me. He turned to Pasquin. "How big are these boats?"

"Not big. 'bout the size of a shrimp boat or one of those cabin boats that can sleep three or four people. You won't get no big steamers up this river."

"Big enough for a good load of fresh Gulf shrimp," I said. I thumped Pasquin's knee. "Maybe this old man will take me up there to see Crawfish Dock one day."

Vernon left for his diving job at the sinkhole. It wouldn't be an easy one in the dark, but the hole was dark anyway, and if they were to gather evidence they had to do it before the item slipped too deeply into the hole or burst open and lost all its contents.

"Are we ready for our jaunt tomorrow morning?" I asked Pasquin as soon as Vernon's car disappeared into the night.

"Yep. I'll come by on the boat around nine. Maybe we'll get there in time to join Gavi for lunch. Raw oysters, perhaps?" He looked my way and laughed. I never ate them that way.

I waved from the porch as I watched Pasquin's old back move into the darkening swamp. He would walk home as he had for years, his swamp compass guiding him without a light. He had become almost mythical to me in his comfort with what most would call a hostile terrain. I wondered if maybe the animals didn't have their own folklore about him, their own reverence for his passage through their territory. Thoughts of cute little cartoon snakes and gators dancing about in a pristine swamp, frogs singing praises as an old man in a straw hat made the trek home made me laugh and shake my head. I knew those snakes were no cartoons, and the bite from just one could lay the old man low on the trail where no one would find him until it was too late.

I walked to my landing where I could look at the dark, quiet river at twilight. Only the occasional splash of a turtle made a sound. As I walked away, I heard the almost silent, rhythmic swish of a boat's wake. On the river, a light shone in the cabin where someone steered a boat upriver.

CHAPTER EIGHT

The water road to oyster country stretched from low scrub-brush sandy soil along the shore to a wide span of ocean bay. Once Pasquin had chugged into the bay and turned toward Apalachicola, the waves were larger and bounced his little boat up and back. Blinding sun rays sparkled off the surface of the open saltwater. In the distance, we saw the small boxy boats, mostly with one occupant who used twelve-foot oyster tongs to lift the shells from the beds. The oyster man leaned slightly over the side, placing the poles attached to metal tongs that looked like two long garden rakes but acted like post hole diggers. The man would open it, lower it into the water, close the tongs and pull out a load of oysters. Water streamed from the grates in the tongs as he dumped the load into the boat. When he had his limit—or in a time of dearth, what he could get—he headed back to one of the shucking houses to sell the live shellfish for a few dollars.

Tradewinds Seafood operated the shucking house that sat at one side of a battered boat dock. The shucking house itself was a plain solid concrete structure. Pasquin tied up his boat on the side of the dock where the oyster boats wouldn't be, and we walked across a mass of oyster shells to the open door of an empty wooden office a few steps away from the shucking house.

Crossing the narrow divide between the office and the concrete house, we pushed aside strips of dirty vinyl that hung over the door to keep out flies. The humidity and powerful odor of oyster fluids hit my nostrils about the same time the screech of the shucking machines hit my eardrums. It seemed torture to make humans stand and work in such a place for any length of time.

Two men and two women stood on concrete platforms beneath the low ceiling in front of four rows of concrete tables divided into concrete cubicles. Each cubicle had a bucket next to its pile of oysters and a red machine the size of a can opener with a cord that reached to a plug in the ceiling. A water hose rested on a hook.

The men wore caps over long hair and the women donned shower caps over their dark braids. In their hands were the flat-bladed, round-handled shucking knives. They kept up a steady routine of breaking the end of the oyster shell against the whining machine, opening and scooping, and dropping the body of the mollusk in the bucket, tossing the shell down a chute that led to the outside of the building, and grabbing the next one.

Gavi was almost unrecognizable in his dirty baseball cap and a make-shift apron that was simply an old flannel shirt tied around his chest, but his toothless grin and his shout over the others took us to a spot near the back of the tiny room. His ancient hand, probably as old as Pasquin's, held an oyster while his other slid the blade between the shell halves where the machine had broken it, scooped out the oyster and deposited it in the bucket.

"How many of those do you eat in a morning?" asked Pasquin.

Gavi laughed, and the next one he scooped out, he dropped it down his throat. "Can't do that much," he said. "Eat up the profits."

I looked around at what must be difficult work that left lingering smells on skin and clothes. "Why are you doing this?" I asked.

"Money. I get some spending stuff. It's easy enough, and I only do it half a day, depending on when the boats come in. Plus, it's only in the season and the seasons ain't been so good lately."

"When you goin' to get off and talk to us?" Pasquin held out his hand, and Gavi handed him the half shell. Pasquin slid the oyster down his own throat.

"You feedin' me?" Gavi yelled over the machines and laughed, his gums showing. Raw oysters would be easy for him.

"Lady Fogarty is picking up this tab. Of course, you got to come up with some information for her."

"Make yourselves a little scarce until I finish this bushel."

Pasquin and I moved down the aisle, dodging the shuckers who concentrated on their work lest they open a hand and not a shell with the pointed blade of the knife. Once in a while, someone would spray running water across a surface to get rid of the sand and oyster debris. The two women didn't look at us. The other man, so gaunt he seemed to have missed several meals, drinking and smoking them instead, had a habit of nodding each time he chunked a naked oyster into his bucket. This was probably the only job he ever knew and the only source of food for his family.

Outside on the dock, quiet soothed our battered eardrums. A man waited next to the oyster chute for the next boat load to arrive. He had a shock of black hair matted by salt air and humidity. His job was to assist the boats bringing in loads by placing them in a water chute that rinsed off mud and bottom debris, culled the small ones out, and weighed them on a scale at the end to determine the amount the boat man would take home that day.

As a boat approached the dock, I was surprised to recognize a man standing near a wall holding a pitchfork. His job, while quiet, was the one requiring the least talent. He raked the shells as the shuckers tossed them down chutes. He would then transport them to a side mound of shells that would be sold for garden borders and calcium pills.

"Patel?" I said as I moved closer to him.

He nodded without saying anything.

"I thought you worked on the shrimp boats."

He turned his back to the other man. "Not too much work on the boats right now. I needed money to pay for that mansion I live in." He gave a sneer on top of a laugh.

"Are you here all day?"

"Could be. Depends on work available. As you can see, I'm not exactly the business suit type. I'll stay longer if I'm needed."

"Where is the manager?"

"Captain Carl? He drifts in and out with a beer until the other boats come in the afternoon. He's got an office over there." Patel nodded toward the wood building, not much more than a shack. Jerking his head back to the task, he said, "Back to work." He hesitated. "Look, don't let on to Corwin Moon that I'm doing this, okay?"

I nodded. It made no difference to me how he paid his bills, but I wondered how a shrimp boat crew job would pay so little that he'd be out of money. Surely, the Moons couldn't be charging much for staying in a crumbling, serve-yourself boarding house.

I followed Pasquin back to the dock.

"You people want something?" the man asked with a marked Hispanic accent.

"Just wondering how you do this," said Pasquin. He stuck out his hand, forcing the man to shake it. "This is Miss Luanne Fogarty, and I'm…"

Before he could finish, a short elderly man in a dirty tee-shirt joined us. "Hey! I know who you are. You found those old ladies in the springs?"

"One old lady in the spring," I said.

"Yeah, well you work for the sheriff, right?" He said it loud enough to be heard over the motor of an arriving boat.

The man stared at me and backed away. His brown eyes opened wide and his mouth uttered something we couldn't hear.

"Sanchez?" His boss moved toward the man. "Are you all right?"

"He looks ill," I said and stepped toward him.

Turning, Sanchez darted toward the end of the dock. He didn't make it. He ran into one of the hoses that cleaned the oyster barrels, causing him to trip and stagger for a moment, one moment too long in the wrong direction. The incoming oyster boat gently bumped the side of the dock, throwing Sanchez into the water between the boat and the dock. The natural momentum of the small boat slammed against the dock and bashed the man's head. He never even screamed.

The manager scrambled to the edge and grabbed Sanchez by the neck of his shirt. Holding as best he could he kicked at the boat, attempting to push it away. When the boat's owner realized what had happened, he guided it from the dock. Sanchez' body was too heavy and the manager was barely hanging on, his hands slipping with water and blood.

"Pasquin! Get people from inside," I said as I jumped into the water next to the dock. The man must have let go then because Sanchez' body slipped and drifted downward. I swam to his legs and wrapped my arms around them. Kicking desperately, I got him partially topside where the two ladies in shower caps grabbed hold of his arm and shoulder, and the male shucker took hold of his clothes as best he could. Sanchez' right arm was dripping blood and seemed nothing but a pole against his side. It may have been crushed, too, but the damage was covered by his clothes. His head lay in a pulp to one side, and one wide brown eye still stared at me.

Everyone moved to the edges of the dock when the ambulance and sheriff arrived. A paramedic kneeled to examine Sanchez with a stethoscope, his white coat dragging in blood made pale by sea water, and pronounced him dead at the scene. From our description of Sanchez' face before he fell, the sheriff's deputy decided it might have been a heart attack that caused him to react like that. He also decided an ME would have to do an autopsy to find out for sure.

Captain Carl appeared anxious, his ruddy face nearly as pale as his apron. An accident on his premises wasn't something he welcomed. "Yes, see if he had a heart attack." He shook hands with the oyster man who owned the boat. "It's not your fault, Mick."

"I know that! What the hell made the man fall off the dock like that?"

The next two hours dragged into those long waits for deputies to question everyone, take statements, addresses, and fire just enough suspicion to make people nervous. We had answered the deputy's questions, gave him our addresses, and were told we were free to leave. That didn't do much for me. I had phoned Manny to tell him I was going to miss my class. On top of that, I had been dripping wet in saltwater for an hour and dried in salt for another.

"Is there a place I can buy some clothes?"

"There's a souvenir place up the road," said Captain Carl. "I've got my truck and can run you up there."

Captain Carl motioned to a worn truck that had Tradewinds Seafood newly painted on the door. I rode with him to a tee-shirt shop that also sold bathing suits, gauze slacks, and lots of Florida memorabilia made in China. After buying a shirt that read "St. George Island" and a pair of drawstring slacks, I changed in a common lavatory room, a separate building behind the shop that looked like a shucking house.

Pasquin had remained on the dock, fanning himself with his hat and chatting with Gavi. They spoke in muffled voices about the accident and agreed that's what it was—just an accident, maybe one that had been brought on by a heart episode, but an accident nonetheless.

Inside the shucking house, work had come to a stop. No one was around, not even the two women. The other man passed us with a dirty duffle bag over one shoulder and said the women took off on foot about as fast as they could go.

"We're still going to lunch, right?" said Gavi.

I dumped my salty clothes into Pasquin's boat and followed him to Gavi's beat-up truck. It seemed as old as he was, but re-markably, air conditioned. He bounced us down two dirt roads before stopping in front of a wooden structure on stilts next to an estuary. The bottom looked like new lumber, a sign that the place had been ruined in a hurricane surge and rebuilt on insur-ance money. A dancing shrimp graced a sign in front, but I never did see a name for the place. Gavi said they had planned to call it "Blown Away," but got scared that such a name might jinx it again.

I stood outside the cafe and phoned my department.

"Iris was actually here in the office when you called," said Manny, gushing admiration for the venerable linguist. "She came by to visit you, and since you couldn't be here, she offered to take your class."

"She took the class? How did she know what to teach?"

"She didn't. Said she was too far behind in the latest stuff, but she could talk to your class about aspects of careers in the field."

"You okayed that? Guest speaker or something?"

"Without pay." Manny laughed. "She said she'd love to do it."

Without speculating on what this long retired lady might tell the impressionable youth of the department, I headed inside and sat down with two old venerables from the swamp world.

The fare was beach Southern—meaning saltwater fish with cornmeal batter, hush puppies, and cheese grits. They made fries here, but only tourists ordered them.

"And you can get greens with your fish," Gavi said, grinning to show why he'd like the soft vegetables instead of the usual slaw.

The cook and his waitress served us in spite of the two o'clock closing time for lunch. They had questions about the accident at the shucking house.

"You can't trust people from somewhere else," said the waitress. "They don't know our boats. It likely spooked him."

"Likely, he was spooked before he knew the boat was there," said Pasquin. He pointed to the mixed fried platter like his old heart never met a thing called cholesterol. Gavi had his heart set on boiled crab dipped in melted butter. I opted for mullet, common and tasty.

"What do you mean 'from somewhere else,'" I asked the waitress.

"Mexicans, I guess. Lots of them come in for the season to work at the shucking houses. Some even take out boats."

"Guess we better do what we came for," said Pasquin. "And it wasn't to fish a dead man from an ocean." With that, it was time to turn away from the death of poor Sanchez. A twinge of sadness ran through me as I surmised he had worked himself into something that paid a few more pennies—culler and weigher and the man who determined the price to be paid—than a common shucker who had to listen to machine screeches every few seconds.

CHAPTER NINE

I turned to Gavi. "I understand you know something about the Moon family and Moon Island."

"And Moon Lake and Moon loonies," added Gavi with a chuckle.

The drone of his voice began, a sing-song that was traditional in story telling among older folks. This wasn't a story, but most likely exaggerated truth about a family that had been in the area long before Gavi's Portuguese ancestors came into the bay.

"I can't tell you everything, 'cause I don't know it all. The Moons had their ticks, unfriendliness being one of them. My daddy ran a shrimp boat up that way and paid old man Moon dock fees to rest up before going out again. He slept on his boat, but many of the fishermen needed a clean bed after going out for days and fighting the hot Gulf winds. They'd pay old lady Moon to bunk in an area off her kitchen. I think it was built to be a long dining room way back in mule days, when people employed lots of workers and needed a place out of the rain to feed them. Hadn't been used for that, 'cept once in a while, even when I was a kid. Same thing went on for years, 'til I became an old man and set up my own place a few miles away. Didn't see much of the Moons after that." He looked up and grinned, "Lots of stars, though. I see those at my camp all the time."

The mullet I ate had been netted out of the ocean that morning. Its soft flesh cooked in light cornmeal was everything a fish eater could hope for, and the hush puppies had just the right fluffy centers to crispy crusts. I dipped one in a red sauce and tried to push Gavi in the direction I wanted to hear.

"Who lived on Moon Island when you were growing up?"

"Mr. and Mrs. Moon, of course. That's the old lady who still lives there. They had a bunch of kids, can't remember how many. Girls who never smiled and boys who always did. Funny how that went. Even when I got to liking girls, I could never get one to look my way. And, I had teeth back then."

Pasquin laughed. "Teeth and fleshier arms, I bet."

"Hell! I was a good lookin' Portugee! 'Course that might have been the trouble. My family were Popers. Moons were something like Baptists."

"Popers? You mean Catholics?"

Gavi nodded and pulled a gold chain from his shirt. It had a small cross at the end, one that needed a good jewelry cleaner.

"Been wearin' this since my Grandpa gave it to me."

Pasquin took a loud sip of the beer he had ordered. "What do you mean something like Baptists?"

"You know, that religion where they yell and holler and beat drums in church." Gavi smiled. "Wouldn't no priest ever put up with noise like that."

"I guess we'd call them Holy Rollers?" asked Pasquin.

"Yeah. The Moons liked to scream at God about their sins. Guess they had so many, He didn't hear about them."

"Like what?" I asked.

"Made them poor girls work like pack mules on that place," he said. "Had them shucking oysters, packing shrimp, cooking, washing, mopping those old boards."

"I don't suppose they ever went swimming?"

"Swimming! Not on your life. Old lady Moon wouldn't have her daughters in a bathing suit. Old man went along with it. Now, mind you, he weren't no anti-woman or anything like that. Went off and juked with some pretty lowlifes many a night. He just wouldn't have no man touching his offspring."

"But they got married," I said.

"After he went nuts in the head," said Gavi, pointing at his temple with a crab claw. "Sat around singing hymns and stuff. Drove his family crazy. Old lady Moon told him to go soak his head in the sinkhole more than one time."

"And he finally did it?" I looked at him and wondered if the light-hearted attitude about marital strife hadn't been more of a domestic war.

Gavi shrugged. "Who knows? That's the rumor. That he just went out there and jumped in and never came up again. 'Course the only person who said that was his woman. Most likely she never wanted him to come up again."

"If he was all that religious, wouldn't he reject suicide?"

"Maybe he heard God calling him from the depths of that hole," said Gavi. "Or maybe the devil."

"Could be the old lady is feeling a bit of guilt now that she's old enough to meet her Maker," said Pasquin.

"She keeps hearing him, or something like that," I said. "She says there are sighs during the night. Sissy said she heard them, too."

Gavi looked down at his plate and gave a "hee-hee" old man's laugh. "Sighs? Probably that pothead they got living there got him a woman."

Pasquin waved a crooked finger at him. "I thought women

and pot didn't work together." He stifled a laugh.

"Okay, both of you calm down. If Trukee were bringing in women, Sissy would have known it. Since she's a pretty independent little cuss, she'd charge the woman for the room."

"How do you know about the pothead?" asked Pasquin.

"The whole damn bay knows about him," said Gavi. "He can pull a draw on one of them handmade cigs and load up a net full of shrimp at the same time. Stuff might make him feel good, but it don't give him impairments." He leaned over the table and giggled again. "Nowhere, no impairments."

I turned to Pasquin. "Do you know if there's any dredging going on in the swamps near the island? I could swear I heard noise from one when we were there one night."

"Might be. I'll ask around. You're thinking that's the sigh the old lady is hearing?"

I nodded. "It's not all in her mind. Sissy heard it, too."

"Lots of development going on around the area. I'll bet them real estate developers would love to get their hands on the Moon house." Pasquin dipped a hush puppy into hot sauce.

"There were other people who visited the Moon house when you were growing up, like the cousin, Rachel Moon. Tell me about her." I said this to focus their minds in another direction.

"Oh, my goodness, Rachel Moon," said Gavi and leaned back, the smile gone from his face. "Now that was one spooked child."

"Spooked?"

"She was dropped off at the Moon house while her own parents took off for somewhere else. Why they never took her, I don't know, but maybe they needed time out from child raising." He swirled his grits, mixing in the cheese. "She was a bit spoiled, one of those kids who cried to get her way. Kept doing that even when she was almost a teen. Her boy cousins teased her some, 'cept when old man Moon made them stop. He'd put his arm around her little shoulders and tell her to go comb her pretty hair."

"She had pretty hair?" asked Pasquin, who swiped a hush puppy off my plate and ran it through the hot sauce.

"Long, curly, red. It shined in the sunlight. Now, that's not something I noticed right away. Not until I heard old Moon say something to one of his daughters that was downright mean."

After a silence that lasted too long while he added butter to his cheese grits, I said, "You're making us wait deliberately, aren't you?"

"Mean, downright mean to tell your own daughter she had drab hair and to go brush it so it'd look more like Rachel's."

"And did the daughter have drab hair?"

"Not to me. Long and red, too. It didn't curl but went straight down."

Gavi talked on and on about running his father's boat by Moon Island, tying up there and going swimming with the Moon boys. Sometimes they swam in the lake, sometimes in little inlets off the boat path. The girls never went in, except for Rachel. She owned a bathing suit and her parents told her to swim for the exercise. She did, but not with the boys. She waited until they left or went early while they were still working on boat jobs. Gavi said he'd sometimes sit on the deck of his father's boat and watch Rachel come around the lake to the sandy shore. She'd slip off a towel she had wrapped around her body—a bit more meat on her than girls you see these days—and slip into the water.

"She'd push off silent as a tadpole, move her arms in a gentle way while she swam into the middle and back. Then she'd slip under the water and cruise around where I couldn't see her. But she always came up near shore again. When she stood up, that long red hair was wet and hung past her waist. She'd stand there in that wet yellow bathing suit and stoop over to wring out her hair." He laughed and turned to me.

"How old was she about that time?"

He looked at the ceiling and closed his eyes like he was thinking. "I figure around fourteen. I'd have been around mid-twenties or so."

"And you never tried to court her?" Pasquin shook his head and laughed.

"Old man Moon would have shot me if I'd dawdled around his cute little cousin. I often wondered if her parents hadn't left some money for her upkeep during the two weeks. He sure protected her and lots more than his own daughters."

"How long did she continue to go there during summers?" I asked.

Gavi stopped smiling and shook his head. "That was it, I think. I didn't see her much after that. Maybe near the springs I'd catch a glimpse of her going somewhere with her mama, but far as I know, she found somewhere else to go after that time."

"Maybe she got tired of the place spooking her," Pasquin laughed.

"More like those boys teasing her. Old man Moon wasn't around anymore to protect her, so maybe she just said I'm not going. You know how stubborn teens can be."

"That's when Mr. Moon went into the lake and never came up again?"

"Yep. So they say. 1959. I kind of doubt it, of course, but that's what his wife said and wouldn't nobody come up with a different story."

"Wouldn't?" I asked and pushed my plate towards Pasquin who was now picking off pieces of mullet.

"Most everyone outside the family figured he'd up and found

him a sweet thing, hopped a boat, and took off for new country."

"Abandonment," Pasquin nodded. "Embarrassing back then."

"What about Mrs. Moon? Did she share in the protection of Rachel while she was there?"

"Now that's something," said Gavi. "That woman was a shrew if ever there was one. Didn't much like her own daughters, or at least never showed them any mothering that I could tell. She sniffed her nose at Rachel." He laughed and dipped the last of his crab into the butter. "Rachel just sniffed back, I think."

"Was Mrs. Moon a shrew to her husband, too?" Pasquin sipped on iced tea.

"Not sure if she yelled at him the way she did the kids, but she sure never smiled much. Maybe inside the house she let him have it. Probably did. That's why most people never got disturbed about his leaving."

"So Mrs. Moon just made up a story about her husband drowning in the lake—possibly committing suicide?"

Gavi shrugged and swiped at his mouth with a napkin. "She reported it. Had the sheriff out there, but they never found him. Of course, diving equipment and such was pretty scarce. I think they hired some diver off a boat to come in and look."

I smiled. I was such a diver, an adjunct originally hired because I knew the spring caves from childhood. The current department was state-of-the-art, latest gear and techniques, along with top notch photographic equipment.

Gavi saluted us like a sailor when he dropped us back at the shucking house dock. The place was locked up tight. We had to walk around the pile of shells to get onto the dock and into Pasquin's boat.

"It'll be pretty dark by the time we pull into your landing," he said as he guided the small boat into the bay.

"Pitch dark if you move at your usual pace." I leaned back and took a last look at the rough boards of the oyster dock. It would do for an artist's subject, maybe a painter or a photographer. A pelican sat on one of the pilings until he spied something and glided along the top of the water. The water shined in the sun that was moving pretty far west, and nothing but the gentle lap of water against Pasquin's boat made a noise. We moved without much bounce through serene twilight waters. Who would have suspected someone's head had been crushed against that little dock?

We chugged along at a steady rate without saying a word for nearly three miles. I think I dozed once or twice. When I awoke, I hoped Pasquin hadn't done the same and got us off course.

"What do you think, old man," I said. "Is Mr. Moon at the bottom of a sinkhole or in bliss with some old lady in Montana?"

"He'd be pretty old by now. The bliss would have fizzled. Most likely he would have, too. Now, if he went into the sink, his bones may be out here in the bay somewhere if they got through all those cave connections. Been too long to find anything."

"It could happen, you know. Bones have lasted a long time in cold water. Provided they haven't moved too deep, we could find them buried down there." I smiled. "Not too likely, huh?"

"Sure is strange why the old lady keeps saying he went in the lake by himself."

"And never came up again." I tried singing a made-up song. Old Man Moon went down into the water and never he rose again.

"Now, Luanne, the moon always rises again. A month later maybe, but it never, ever stays down."

The real moon did us a favor and rose enough to guide us back to the Palmetto River. Several boats passed us on their way back from all day fishing trips. Sunburned city people rested in deck chairs, weary of the salt air. They headed for pretty houses on stilts near the section of the river that joined the bay. We moved on through the dark waters to my landing.

"You want to come in for tea?" I asked Pasquin who had begun slapping at mosquitoes with his straw hat.

"I got to get home," he said. "I'm weary to the bone. Best you do the same."

I listened to his boat motor fade as it rounded the bend toward his own landing. Turning toward the house, I spied Plato standing at the bottom step, his tail moving faster and faster. He wasn't barking. When I looked on the porch, I saw Vernon open the screen door and head my way.

"I thought I was going to have to leave a note for you," he said. He took my clothes that now felt like gritty paper from the saltwater. "What's this? Are you collecting for the needy?"

"I took a swim, but I wouldn't call it a pleasure dip."

"I heard," he said, his face not smiling.

"What did you hear?"

"Some shucker fell off the dock, hit his head, and died at the spot."

"Law enforcement news travels fast. I didn't realize another county would convey an incident like that."

"They can't find the man's family or his address. Seems the one he gave the company was a motel room."

"And they couldn't find anyone who knew him there?"

"There is no 'there' there," he said. "It was a motel that closed years ago and is on the verge of falling down. If he lived there, he did it without amenities and with all the other tramps."

CHAPTER TEN

The moon shone brightly now, putting Plato in a ghostly light at the top of the stairs. Having time to think on the boat trip home gave me an uneasy feeling. Sanchez not only died a brutal death, he disappeared into the vapors.

"Just like Mr. Moon," I said.

"Like who?" Vernon held the door for me, tossing the clothes into a rocking chair.

"Moon, the man who walked into the lake and vanished."

"You're still on him?" Vernon smiled that cryptic way that turned up the corners of his lips but went no further.

"It's pretty intriguing, you have to admit," I said.

"Especially when his little descendant is at your door every day."

"Not every day."

"She came here about two hours ago." He gazed down at me, then leaned over to scratch Plato's ears.

"Sissy was here? What did she have to say this time?"

"I was sitting on your porch when I heard a boat pull up to the dock. It didn't sound like Pasquin's boat but I figured that's whose it was. I started to come down the steps when that scraggly swamp girl crossed the road. She took one look at me and ran like hell back to her boat."

"You didn't go after her?"

"Sort of—at least I walked on the landing in time to see her move into the river. Her little boat chugged along as fast as she could get it to move."

I stopped to pet Plato who was now sniffing out oyster vapors. They had to be on my skin because the clothes were new.

"I wonder what she wanted."

"You're not going over there at this hour?"

I grabbed him by his collar and pulled him after me into the house. "No, but I am going to ask you why you're here."

We fell on the sofa together, and for the first time in days, his arms went around me. For a few seconds I forgot about screeching oyster machines that broke off the shell ends, rendering the mollusk defenseless and ready to be knifed and plucked from its thick, irregular fortress.

"First tell me about the questioning when this man Sanchez fell to his death."

I looked up at him. He wasn't smiling. Any little episodes of bed play were going to have to wait for business, it seemed.

After I had once again relayed all I knew, he sat silently.

"You know," I said, "those two women were Hispanic, too. They may have known Sanchez and where he lived. Sometimes people use nicknames. Maybe Sanchez is just what they call him."

"Sometimes people take other names because they don't want others to know who they really are." He gently placed two fingers over my lips when I began to protest. "We can't find the two women, either."

"We?"

"The two sheriff's departments." He paused and removed his arms. "You told me about Sanchez, the other male shucker, Captain Carl, Gavi, the two Hispanic women. Besides you and Pasquin, was there anyone else about the place?"

I eyed him carefully, but he wouldn't look at me. "Something else is going on here, right?"

Vernon said nothing, just lifted his eyebrows to let me know he was waiting for an answer.

"Let's see." I closed my eyes and tried to remember the place as it had been when we entered. "Empty office, four shuckers, Sanchez, and… the tossed shells! Patel! He had a job of raking up the tossed shells and putting them on the pile at the side."

"Patel, yes. We haven't found him, either."

"He wasn't around when the deputies came. I guess I forgot about him, figured his job was done and he had gone home."

"Were the shells raked up?"

I hadn't looked because we thought the death was an accident. I had been distracted by my sticky, itching clothes and I'd wanted nothing more than comfort at the time. "Damn! It's not like me to be careless about things like that."

"You were there to find out about the Moon family, right?"

"That's why I was surprised to see Patel there. He said he needed the extra money."

"Extra change, more likely." Vernon stood up, pulled out his cell phone and moved to the porch. From his tone, I knew he was speaking to someone about law enforcement. "Anything turn up yet? Nothing here, either. Later." He folded the phone and tucked it in his pocket. His smile indicated an attitude change, and he grabbed me for a hurried cuddle.

"Damn, woman, oyster doesn't make a nice perfume."

"I'll shower," I said. "Don't you go anywhere."

I ran upstairs to my bathroom. When I looked back, Vernon was on his cell phone again.

The moment was hurried, a desire that needed satiating. The touches and kisses ran hard and furious, and we accidently moved the bedding to the floor with eager body movements. It ended with a laugh.

Vernon grabbed his watch from the side table.

"I've got to run."

"No dinner?"

He shook his head. "Sorry. I'm on the job." He looked at me with the sheepish little boy stare that said he wanted to say something but wanted no criticism in return.

"What?"

"Maybe sometime tomorrow, after your classes, of course, you and Pasquin could take a ride to Moon Island. Call me if Patel shows up."

"Is he wanted for something?"

Vernon half smiled, tweaked my chin and said he'd check with me later. I followed him downstairs still naked. He leaned and kissed both breasts. At the door, he gave Plato's ear a jerk and headed away from me.

I sat in the dark living room, a throw tossed around my body. Plato rested his wiry face on my feet, thumping his tail on the floor to let me know he was still there and needed attention. My irritation at being patronized ground at my ego. If Vernon couldn't talk, I told myself, I had to let it be. After all, I wasn't telling him everything, either.

"What's going on, boy?" I rubbed his ears. He rolled on his back and let me scratch his tummy. "You want to eat?"

I tied the throw around me and we retreated to the kitchen

where I opened a can of food for Plato, and made a hamburger and coleslaw for myself. About the time I finished, Iris came to mind. I picked up the phone to see if my students had worn out the old lady.

"Worn out! Dear, I loved it!" She had answered the phone as though sitting right over it. "Being with the youthful spirits just takes me back."

"They showed interest in the field, then?"

"Had all sorts of questions. I told them about field work, about meeting with tribes as well as city cultures. Now," her voice lowered, "I tried to tell them about forensic linguistics but I have no experience there. Only what I see on the television and have read in a few articles. Oh, there were lots who wanted to go that direction."

"No history buffs?" I was joking. It was obvious that modern crime detection was the draw with this particular class. Studying the origins of modern languages took a back seat.

"A few. One fellow wants to study the Viking dialects and how they relate to English."

"Speaking of dialects, I need to go back to Moon Island tomorrow. You want to go?"

"Just tell me where to meet you!" Iris sounded excited..

"I've got to recruit a neighbor of mine to take us in his boat. Are you still okay with boats?"

"Honey, you saw what I've got stashed away in a shed behind my house. One day I need to pull one out and get it refurbished to go somewhere."

We agreed to meet at the dock in Fogarty Spring the next day. Iris would drive herself, something she said she would do until her brain withered and her old ankles refused to push her foot to the pedal. "Old age just isn't going to take it all away from me yet."

Pasquin whined a bit, but the idea of nosing into Moon Island again was too much temptation for him to refuse. He would pick us up at the Fogarty Spring dock, which I thought would be an easier place for Iris to climb into a boat.

After that was settled, I changed into shorts and a big shirt and sat in a chair on the front porch while Plato chewed on a thick beef bone beyond the steps. The night seemed to sing out of the darkness. Every critter voiced its pleasure or pain in the feeding frenzy beneath a full moon. I leaned back in the rocker and gazed into the sky. The silver white orb was farther up now and would eventually move behind the house. I'd have to go to the other side to see it. Was it true that people went a little crazy during a full moon? Hospitals say that emergency rooms tend to fill. They were full most of the time anyway. Did old Mrs. Moon hear her husband's sighs more tonight than at other times? Would she wander around outside and stare into the lake, maybe seeing her husband's eyes looking up at her? Poor Sissy would have to run after her before she fell in and joined the old man. "But he ran off with a cutie, didn't he?" I said it loud enough for Plato to stop gnawing and look up at me. When he realized there was no alarm, he wagged his tail twice and turned back to the bone.

I let the humidity and swamp noises surround me until I began to doze. Somewhere in my consciousness I felt I should get up and go to bed knowing I'd be bitten alive by mosquitoes otherwise.

I didn't move until I heard the muffled engine. It was coming from the bay side of the river, moving north. I rose from the rocker and walked toward the landing. A light appeared down the river and became brighter. The boat was a shrimper, its rigging sticking up like leaning flag poles. It would normally carry about six or eight shrimpers who would take turns sleeping in the bunks below deck. A dim light burned from below this deck. Someone stood in the pilot's cabin, but I couldn't see anyone else. When Plato gave out a sharp bark, the pilot turned to see the two of us standing on the landing. He pulled off his hat and tipped it toward me. I gave a half wave back to him. "Night deliveries, do you think?" Plato barked again and trotted back to his bone.

Iris' enthusiasm prevailed in my class the next morning. It was clear that my students were in awe of her.

"She actually paddled her own canoe and interviewed swamp rats," said one young man. "Lucky she wasn't skinned along with the possums."

"And she can speak to some of the Seminoles in south Florida," said a chubby girl with red hair. "I want to do that."

When the gushing stopped, a serious girl who sat in the back row raised her hand. "Iris said she'd take us on a field trip if we wanted to go."

"Where?" I felt an alarm go off inside. This woman would surely need someone to help her take these beginners into the wilderness.

"She didn't say. Just to a place where the language is peculiar to the area and follows the profession. She said if we had any ideas to tell you."

I smiled, all the while dreading the thought of herding thirty post-teens onto a bus or a boat and dragging them into a closed community of suspicious people who may never have even graduated high school. It wasn't the way linguists were supposed to work.

"We'll see," I said. "First, you have to master phonetics in order to understand the sounds the people will make when they speak."

By the end of my afternoon class that included most of the morning class, I'd heard enough praise of Dr. Iris Henderson to give her a lifetime award for bravery. Now, I had to take her into the field.

I changed into jeans and tee-shirt in my office and hurried off to Fogarty Spring. I pulled up in front of Mama's Table. As I suspected, Iris was there. She wore overalls and a long sleeved tee "to ward off the noseeums" she said. Iris sat on the bottom step of the cafe entrance, sipping iced tea. Mama, whose heavy body and bad knees refused to sit her on the steps, leaned against the railing and sipped her own tea.

"You're right on time!" said Iris. She motioned for me to join them. I sat behind her to avoid blocking the way for customers. The day was waning and fishermen would be stopping in soon.

"Old man Pasquin isn't," said Mama. "Never is."

"He'll be here. Just takes him a while to get going at his age."

"Now, let's avoid that subject," laughed Iris.

I shook my head. "We won't be able to when you meet Mrs. Moon. She's close to ancient."

"Great! I want to talk to all generations of Moons and anyone who has lived in the area for years. You know the routine, Luanne, I record what they say and look for recurring patterns." She pulled out a small recorder from a huge leather bag that sat on the step between her feet. "Faithful little fellow."

"How many recorders have you been through in all your years?"

"Not so many. I only changed when they made a better one. One got stolen on a camping trip once. I figured one of the teens wanted it." She cocked her head and smiled. "I wonder if he's still got it and gets a pang of guilt every time he comes across it."

"Not if he's sitting in jail," said Mama. She raised her tea glass to ask if I wanted some.

"Pasquin is coming," I said. "Better bring out two glasses. In fact, pack some fish sandwiches. I don't know what we'll find on Moon Island."

Pasquin loaded the bag of sandwiches and some bottled water onto his boat. He had been the gallant old gentleman when he met Iris, even leaned over to kiss her hand. She gave me a silly grin when he did that. I held the boat steady from the dock while Pasquin took both her hands. She went with remarkable agility into the boat and onto a seat, dragging her leather bag on one arm.

"I'd like to listen to you talk sometime, Mr. Pasquin," she said. "Any chance of that?"

"Listen to me all you want in this boat," he said. His eyes lit up.

"That I'll do, but I have to listen in the same way I'll listen to the Moons."

"How's that?" he asked.

"She has to listen to each person talk about the same subject," I said. "That way, they're likely to use many of the same words and give her a dialect pattern."

"What subject should I ask them about?" Iris said, looking from me to Pasquin.

"How about the family legend about old Mr. Moon," I said.

"A legend! Oh, good. Nothing like it to bring out the old language not influenced by modern television. Are they likely to want to talk about the subject?"

"Old Mrs. Moon," said Pasquin, "will talk your head off about it. Her son not so much. You're going to find it hard to find lots of people."

"Doesn't matter. I'm not looking to publish a paper, just to discover some new things."

"You'll have to approach them as a linguist," I said. "Explain what you're doing. Otherwise, they may think you're a plant, some-one who will report to the sheriff. The old lady won't mind that, but her son, Corwin, will."

"Such fun!" Iris leaned over and pulled out a straw hat with a tie and shoved it on her head. She made a bow beneath her chin and smiled up at Pasquin as he patted his own battered straw over his white hair.

"I'm going to take a little longer way to get there," Pasquin said after about fifteen minutes on the river. "There's a water lane leading into an area just beyond the island. I got something to show you."

I said nothing but silently muttered, *it better be good, old man. We're already short on time.*

In the distance, we could see the tops of the trees on Moon Island. Pasquin began to turn the boat to the left and finally moved into a narrow lane. We couldn't go to the end. There were men with a dredger and some other yellow machinery in operation, moving water and dirt from the lane to a holding pond. One en-gine made an airy sound, like a huge bellows blowing on the devil's fire. This close, it was merely irritating.

"Runs all night, they tell me," said Pasquin. "On Moon Island, it won't be so loud. More like a sigh." He grinned at me.

"Old man's ghost is just a modern machine," I said. "Sissy will be happy to hear that." I shook my head. "I doubt Mrs. Moon will comprehend it."

We turned back to the open river and headed for the island. If Pasquin could find out from his swamp buddies about the origin of the sighs, why couldn't he find out what happened to the old man?

CHAPTER ELEVEN

Sissy stood on the Moon dock and waved to us as we approached. Her stringy hair looked even dirtier than usual. Her feet were bare and covered with mud.

"How did you know to come here?" she asked before we got out of the boat. She didn't take her eyes off Iris, her stare one of accusation and intrusion. "Who's she?"

I made the introductions and said Iris was a great linguist who studied the way people spoke. "She'd like to talk to your grandma, if possible."

Sissy shrugged and finally moved her gaze off Iris.

"Sissy, you came by my house yesterday. What did you need?"

She shrugged again and looked at her feet. "Nothing much. I had to pick up pills for Grandma at Rachel's house. Just stopped by, that's all."

Something in her voice hit a nerve, a sympathetic one. Sissy had a reason, but she wasn't about to reveal it in front of these two old people.

"Look, you take Iris up to your grandma and try to convince her to cooperate. Pasquin can sit with Patel or whomever is around, and you and I can take a walk and talk."

She nodded but never smiled. Her shoulders drooped a moment before she motioned for Iris to follow her.

"Charming," said Iris and trudged up the bank toward the old house.

Before we got to the front steps, Sissy turned to Pasquin and said, "You'll have to sit with Trukee. Patel ain't to home and my father takened a boat out to sea."

Iris' face lit up. "Oh, wonderful! That's just what I need. Darling, you have lovely speech. I hope your grandma talks just the same."

"She does," Sissy stared at the woman, some disdain showing in the frown. "You planning on recording her?"

"How did you know?" Iris pulled out the recorder. "It's so little, she won't even notice. Doesn't even make a clicking sound."

"She might be ornery. I ain't takened up her supper yet."

"Does she like fish sandwiches?" I asked.

"She likes what all I bring her. You got some?"

Pasquin chuckled and turned back to the boat. He joined us on the porch with the bag that Mama had packed. Mrs. Moon was going to get the best fish sandwich she'd had in months.

Mrs. Moon took one look at Iris and grinned from her raggedy chair in her bedroom. Iris spoke to her in a gentle tone and shook her hand. She even explained what she wanted to do and how she wanted it recorded.

"You want to hear me talk?" Mrs. Moon's coarse voice asked, but there was a bit of a thrill behind it.

"Yes. I want to make a record of your words, tone, and usage. We think there may be a unique way of speaking on this island."

"Of course there is!" Mrs. Moon smiled now, a broad grin, happier than I'd ever seen her. "The Moons are special."

"Good! We'll eat first." Iris passed the woman a sandwich.

Sissy closed the door, and I followed her back downstairs to the grimy living room. Pasquin found a seat on the front porch, put his hat over his face, and slept, or pretended to. No one ever knew what he did beneath that old relic of tattered straw. Trukee was nowhere in sight.

"Have a sandwich," I said and passed one to Sissy. She ate it ravenously.

"Does Rachel feed you when you pick up the pills?"

She shrugged. "Sometimes. If she's in a hurry to go somewhere, she'll give me a dollar to buy something."

"A dollar doesn't buy much these days."

She shrugged again and offered no explanation of what she did to put nourishment in her scrawny body.

"You wanted to talk?" I passed over bottled water. After gulping a few swallows, she nodded.

"I wanted to know if you knew anybody who might come and rent a room here. Patel left, and we need the money."

"Where did he go?"

Sissy gave her despondent shrug, a talent she was cultivating.

"How do you know he's gone and not just out on a job?"

"He always told us and paid up to hold the room. He didn't do that this time."

"Does he have any personal stuff in the room?"

Sissy looked at me, her eyes questioning my trust.

"I looked a little, just to make sure he's gone. He takened all his clothes out of the closet and there's no billfold anywhere."

"Inside the dresser?"

"Just a little table with a drawer in there, but it's empty, too."

I rested against the ragged furniture and thought about Vernon asking about Patel. This is why he wanted me to return to Moon Island today, to see if Patel showed up here. It was more than just wanting to question him about Sanchez' accident.

"Sissy, could I see the room?"

She held up her hand to say wait until she finished her sandwich. When she'd had every crumb and licked her fingers of tartar sauce, she waved her hand. I followed her up the stairs.

Patel had a room on the end, meaning he had two windows, one facing the front yard and one facing the side where he could see mostly forest. The door wasn't locked. It had an ancient bolt inside, one that looked like it could be kicked open by a small boy. Inside, I was reminded of what I thought a tenement room in a big city would look like: a twin bed consisting of only a frame and a mattress. It had unmade grimy sheets and a chenille spread with tufts missing. The pillow was shoved against the wall. The floor, unswept and sandy, had at one time been shiny wood floors. I opened the closet door, its knob rusted except where the hand gripped it. An odor of mildewed wood brushed by me for a second. Nothing but a few wire hangers and dust on the floor greeted me. Any evidence that Patel had stayed there were gone.

I checked the simple wooden table. It had glass rings where someone had placed a drink and nothing inside its one drawer.

"Where is the bathroom?"

"The boarders share one across the hall." Sissy pointed toward the door. It had swung shut from the tilt of the house. If someone didn't work on this place soon, it would become uninhabitable.

The bathroom could have been a grand old place. It still had a claw foot tub and a pedestal sink. Someone had attached a hand shower to the tub faucet and let the shower head rest on the bottom. The tired linoleum had no design other than footprints, with and without shoes. The toilet, yellowed permanently, resembled a public facility. I opened the medicine cabinet with the tip of my finger.

"There is a shaving kit in here," I said. "Trukee's or Patel's?"

Sissy stood on tiptoes and stared at the razor and can of shaving cream. "Oh man! He forgot these."

"And the toothbrush?" A brush wrapped in some torn cellophane paper rested beside the shaving cream. A rolled tube of toothpaste was behind it.

"Must be his, too."

"Sissy, do me a favor. Leave all this right where it is, okay? I need to talk to someone."

A kid with a precarious life like Sissy's is often wise beyond her years. She didn't know why, but nodded that she'd do as I asked.

"Where's Trukee's stuff?"

"I think he keeps it in his room. Brings it back and forth. I watched him do that a few mornings."

"Do you clean their rooms?"

She shook her head. This was a rent a room as you see it establishment.

"Is Trukee in there now?"

Sissy's radar clicked in again and she waved her hand once more. With the silence of a thief, she opened the door of the room next to Patel's.

Trukee may have taken drugs, and he looked unkempt in person but the bed was made and the floor swept. A small broom rested against one wall next to a dust pan and a trash can. He had a wood table like the one in Patel's room, likely one of a pair, but this one was dusted and free of glass rings. A rectangular plastic box rested on top and held his toiletries. Someone, perhaps Trukee himself, had hung a square mirror on the wall above the table.

I pulled open the drawer to find several pairs of neatly folded underwear.

"Do you have a washing machine here?"

Sissy nodded. "It's behind the kitchen. I do ours, but the boarders do their own."

Inside the closet, clean shirts and jeans hung neatly from wire hangers. A pair of blue and white running shoes rested on the floor, which was clear of dust.

"Did you have any idea he was so clean?"

Sissy smiled. "Sure didn't."

I didn't want to ask in front of a minor but she brought the question up before I could find a way to search.

"I wonder where he keeps his stash?"

I stared at this fragile overworked child. She knew a lot for her age.

It was my turn to shrug. I looked underneath the bed. There was nothing, just clean floor. I went back to the closet and ran my hand over the shelf. Two copies of old *National Geographic* magazines rested there, but nothing else.

"Well, if he has a stash, he's got it on him."

We left the room, both of us silent with our thoughts of how odd this was. Trukee, the guy who sat on the porch, unable to converse because he was high and looking like a time warp from the 1960s, was neat as a pin.

"Just let this be our secret for now, okay?" I said as I followed Sissy downstairs. When we passed Mrs. Moon's room, we could hear her nonstop ramble about the house in the old days. I wondered if Iris had convinced her to talk about the legend of her husband's disappearance. It was something everyone had an opinion about, and she'd get repeated words and patterns.

I left Sissy in the downstairs bathroom and went into the front yard to phone Vernon.

"Some of his stuff is still there?"

"And it's stuff he'd need if he had moved out, or even if he planned to be on a shrimp boat for several days."

"I'll join you in about half an hour. I'm in a boat on the bay right now. Stay there." Vernon clicked off. It was unusual for members of the sheriff's department to be in a boat on the bay.

I sat on the bank near the landing and waited for Vernon. The sky was dimming, and it would again be dark before Pasquin got us home. He had roused himself from the sagging porch and roamed around the yard, fanning away bugs, and talking about how the scrub needed to be removed to make the yard pretty again. At one point, he made the comment that the house looked about like old people: warped, wrinkled, and peeled.

"But we oldies know a lot," he said, "and I'll bet this old place knows a great deal of tales." He stopped. The wind was blowing our way, making the sighs from the machinery audible. "Better let Sissy know what that is," he said.

Vernon still hadn't arrived when Trukee came walking through the woods from the direction of the bridge. He carried a large gunny sack over his shoulder. When he saw us, he grinned, showing white teeth amid the beard stubble.

"Look what I got, Miss Sissy."

Sissy had been sitting on the edge of the dock, washing the dried mud from her feet. She stood up to meet him on shore.

Trukee put the bag down at her feet and untied the rope at the opening. A familiar smell drifted through the air and dissipated. Pasquin and I joined Sissy to stare into a black mass of irregular stones at the bottom.

"Oysters!" Sissy did a dance, looking happy like a child should, and grabbed one from the sack. "I've got a rock we use and some knives," she said. "We love these things."

She took off for the house. Trukee pulled up the bag and slung it across his shoulder.

"Love making that kid happy," he said and trudged after her.

"Oysters?" I looked at Pasquin.

"Looks like he harvested them himself."

CHAPTER TWELVE

Vernon arrived to see Pasquin and me sitting on the dock. Iris and Mrs. Moon were still talking by the light that now shined from the upstairs room. Trukee and Sissy were in the yard behind the kitchen, attempting to crack open and shuck his oysters. It would be pretty hard work without the help of a shucking machine.

"You'd best go upstairs and look in that bathroom now, before Trukee sees you," I said.

In a house that had given up and allowed the elements to encroach, it wouldn't be difficult for a stealthy human to edge himself upstairs, make the rounds of empty rooms, and return with nothing but a palmetto bug being aware of his presence. And that's what Vernon did. He met us on the porch again, his footsteps no louder than some approaching raccoon across the rough boards.

"I got a few things for the lab," he said, and patted his pockets.

"What are you looking for?" I whispered towards him. My frown at being left out must have sent the intended signal.

"Look," he said and sat down on a rickety chair, "Patel is missing. He didn't stay around to answer questions when that oyster man took a fall, and he hasn't shown up here, either. We've contacted the Coast Guard and some other people who go out on the Gulf every day. No one claims to have seen him on one of the shrimp boats." He sighed and held up a hand when I started to ask why they were concerned enough to go to all that trouble. "I can't say right now, but it's vital we find him." He patted his pocket again. "It's kind of strange that none of his things are in his room, but his toiletries are still here."

"Have you asked Trukee?"

"More than once. He hasn't a clue. We saw him on an oyster boat in the bay. He hadn't seen Patel coming this way, and he'd need to get a ride back here somehow."

"A man goes missing in all this water," said Pasquin. "I'd look to a drowning."

Vernon nodded. He glanced around as though the bushes might have ears. "That's going to be the next place we look."

Nothing more could be said because loud footsteps came from inside the house. Mrs. Moon's voice kept up a prattle about how her kids had disappointed her but maybe Sissy would come out all right. She and Iris joined us on the porch.

"Sit here, ma'am," said Pasquin and stood to offer Mrs. Moon his chair.

She stopped talking in midsentence and stared at him. Her eyes moved only to follow his hat as he waved it again toward the chair.

"Are you…no…," she said as she reached out to touch his cheek. Pasquin, the gentleman, leaned toward her and let her feel his rough skin. "I thought for a minute you were…" Her eyes went blank, glazed over as though she was looking inside her mind for a lost image.

Iris saw the action and smiled. She put out her hand to the woman and said, "Mrs. Moon, you have been so kind to let me record all these stories. I have a wealth of material to work with and am so happy you'll see me again." She turned to me. "She even gave me a few names of neighbors who know these stories."

"Got what you came for, then?" I smiled, wondering if Mrs. Moon remembered the last hour with this woman. The names she gave Iris may have been people who faded from existence long ago.

Mrs. Moon's eyes filled with recognition. She turned from Pasquin and shook hands with Iris, smiling and saying "you're welcome…anytime" at least three times. When we all looked as though we were going to leave the porch and head for the dock, she said, "Wait! I want to show you the lake."

Without another word, she pushed me aside and led us all toward the back of the house. When she reached the edge where the bank dropped down abruptly to black water, she said, "This is where he went off. Just under this old oak. Moved out like this and fell into the water." She took a step toward the edge but pulled back, to our relief.

I stood near her in case she decided to take a swim herself. The ancient oak that grew there put out low hanging branches, full of heavy moss. I looked toward the house and from this position; I could only see the top floor.

"You were standing at that window?" I asked and pointed to the one that would have had the best view.

"Yes, just there." Her eyes went dreamy again and she stared at the window, her head crooked at an odd angle.

I tried to imagine myself in that window, gazing down at the lake and being able to see only one shore. If this old oak was anywhere near its current size, I'd have seen lots of leaves and moss but no one who stood underneath. The branches nearly touched the high bank. Anyone coming from beneath the tree would be visible only when he reached the edge.

"Mrs. Moon," I said and nudged her elbow. "Was there anyone else out here that day? I mean swimmers, like the kids who swim today on the other side?"

She turned her head slowly toward mine and realization took some seconds before reappearing. "I didn't see anyone at the time. Lots of young boys were out earlier, but they'd all takened off somewhere."

"That's just what she said on tape," said Iris, "used that same form for took. Great stuff!" She patted the recorder now tucked beneath one arm.

Before we could reach further into Beatrice Moon's brain for more of that infamous day in 1959, a voice called from the far side of the lake.

"Yo! Look who I brought home." It was Corwin, his overalls stained with the products of three days of shrimping. He hadn't shaved during that time, and he wore a battered cowboy hat. Next to him, a shorter version walked with his head lowered.

"Who's that?" Mrs. Moon clasped a hand to her mouth and opened her eyes wide. She stared into the trees as though seeing a ghost.

"It's your grandson, Corwin, and someone else," I said.

Iris moved next to the woman and clasped her elbow. Mrs. Moon looked at her in bewilderment. "Is it…" She gasped again and grabbed hold of Iris. "…Oscar?"

"It's Corwin, Grandma, my daddy," a young voice shouted from behind us. "He's come back and brought Uncle Aaron with him." She frowned and put her hands on her hips. This was not an uncle she would greet joyfully. "I guess he got out of jail."

Mrs. Moon looked as though all knowledge of the world just left her. She slid down Iris' side and sat on the grass. Her eyes stared straight ahead without realizing she was looking at two of her closest relatives walking towards her.

"What's the matter now?" said Corwin. He went toward his grandmother and bent over to look into her eyes. "Sissy. Take her upstairs."

Sissy handed me the small oyster knife she had been using, and pulled her great-grandmother by her sleeve.

"And while you're at it, put some clean towels in Aaron's room. He'll be here for a while."

"Lucky us," Sissy said under her breath. In a louder voice, she answered her father with, "Hope you brought some food. Patel is gone and we won't have his rent money."

"Gone?" Corwin looked at her for a moment. "We got some bags of shrimp."

"Great. Trukee brought some oysters. Looks like we'll be shellin' and eatin' seafood." Her reply sounded cynical and very grown up.

I looked at the oyster knife with its short, flat pointed blade with a rounded wood handle, the stickiness from oyster juice clinging to my palm. Watching Sissy walk the old lady back to the house, I saw Trukee appear in the distance. He carried a plastic bucket filled with gray water and what must have been shucked oysters.

"You go on up," Corwin said to his brother. "I'll get the bags." He started to turn back towards the side of the lake where larger boats could tie up, but stopped and faced me.

"Just what are you doing here?"

"I came with Dr. Iris Henderson here. She's studying the spoken dialect used on and around this island."

He stared at Iris for a moment and laughed, "We don't talk no different from your local redneck swamp rat, ma'am."

"Well, yes, you do, a bit," Iris smiled at him. "It's all so interesting. I'd like to record you someday, if I may."

"Record me? I never takened to singing."

"Oh, lovely! I want your speech, and you just confirmed your dialect."

Corwin looked perplexed, shrugged and walked into the trees.

With no one left, I turned but couldn't see Vernon anywhere. Pasquin had retreated to a tree where he leaned against the trunk and fanned away mosquitoes.

"You ready to leave this locale?" he said and did a half bow to Iris.

"Mr. Pasquin, you must let me record you sometime, too."

"Me! I don't talk like these Moonbeams."

"No, you have an idiolect, a special way to speak all your own." Iris grinned at him.

"Now I'm an idiot, and an old one at that." Pasquin slammed his hat on his head. "Get in the boat and let's get out of this place. We're all going crazy. I'll be seeing people walk off into sinkholes pretty soon."

"Where's Vernon?" I asked him before Iris caught up to us.

"Snuck off soon as he heard that man call from the woods. Said he'd contact you at your house and that I was to get you back there right now."

There were no good-byes to Sissy or her grandmother. I looked back once and saw Corwin hauling in some clear plastic bags at the back of the house. Otherwise, it was like the entire Moon entourage had disappeared within the old walls.

We loaded ourselves and Iris' recorder back into Pasquin's boat and let him chug chug us back to Fogarty Spring. Iris talked most of the way about how she had Beatrice repeat the story of Oscar's demise over and over again.

"She didn't seem to realize she was repeating it," she said. "Poor dear has all the signs of encroaching Alzheimer's or some kind of dementia."

"Or just madness from that one incident," said Pasquin. "People do that, go mad from something awful and never get their brains in order again."

"She seemed so happy to tell me about the event. Not that she was happy she lost her husband, but that it was something exciting."

I looked at Pasquin who guided the boat around clumps of floating river grass. "Is there any chance she's faking it?"

Pasquin looked at me for a while, until his face broke into a chuckle. "Now wouldn't that be something. Faking her craziness."

"Oh no," said Iris. "I've seen too many people her age with mental problems. She's not faking it. She's proud of something, but I don't know what. The story excites her, puts life in her eyes."

I sat up and stared at Iris, her frizzy hair whipping about her wrinkled face in the slight breeze the forward movement of the boat was making. "Is there any possibility, Iris, that she did away with the old man herself?"

Iris shrugged and broke into a belly laugh. Pasquin joined her, and their voices echoed down the river, causing anhinga birds to take flight from cypress knees.

It was close to dark by the time we reached the dock at Fogarty Spring. Mama's Table still had its lights on, and Iris was not ready to call it an evening.

"This is the most excitement I've had in years," she said as she climbed out of the boat, one hand grasping Pasquin's. "I'm as hungry as a bear and I'm going to treat you both." Not an invitation but a demand. Neither of us protested.

"You'll not have much choice this evening," said Mama as she limped to our table. "Had lots of customers in here earlier. Just about ate up the ocean." She bent over and rubbed her knee. "Old thing is bothering me today."

Iris took over and ordered seafood platters all around, demanding the check be brought to her.

"Tell me," I said to Mama, "how often do you have strangers in here or foreigners?"

Mama took the question as a cue to sit down. Her hefty body placed itself on a chair dragged from another table, and her face seemed relieved.

"Sometimes. I've seen the men who work on the shrimp boats in here. Chinese and Indians and some others. Even a couple of Swedes with that sweet accent. They must have a time of it in this humid weather, coming from a cold country. Good looking fellows, tall and blond."

"Fishermen, just the same," said Pasquin.

"And what's wrong with that, Old Man? I sell fish, make my living off them. Don't tell me I can't praise the looks of the fellows that haul them in here." She glared at Pasquin, who smiled and dipped a fried shrimp into a hot sauce she made special for him.

"Does Corwin Moon ever eat here?" I asked.

"Not often. I see him when he's delivering on the river."

"He delivers shrimp?"

Mama nodded. "Stops here sometimes and drops off a bag. Not much, but enough to keep me in supply for a day. Best part is, he charges less than the other boats."

"Does his cousin ever join him?"

"Rachel? Ha! She won't come in here. Says fishermen aren't nice people and she has no plans to eat with them. Far as I know, she has nothing to do with that cousin of hers. He eats, delivers his goods, turns around and heads back to the boat."

Iris, eager to be part of the conversation, picked up a grouper finger with her fork and announced, "And she's missing a treat. This is the best!"

Mama stared at her and finally grinned, her chubby cheeks folding back to her tiny ears with minute diamond studs. "I'll tell you something. That Rachel likes it, too. Once in a while she'll call here and have food for her girls delivered. Wouldn't let those kids come near the place, but she lets them eat the food."

"Mustn't let the boogeyman shrimper get near the little kids," said Pasquin. "No wonder the old broad never married."

"Old broad, never married?" I said and glared at him.

"Now, ma'am, some of us are still marryin' age." His face reddened. It was his old argument that I wouldn't last in this cruel world without a husband. I was proving him wrong as each year passed.

"Do you know if this Rachel speaks like the other Moons?" asked Iris.

"Speaks like them?" Mama looked surprised. "I guess so. I'd be able to identify her as a Moon if I heard her over the phone."

"Yes!" Iris clapped her hands twice like a little girl. "That's exactly what I needed to hear. You don't know why, but you know it's a Moon way of talking. That means she uses the same dialect and probably intonation."

"What are you talking about?" Mama's face took on a distrust of this childlike elderly specimen in front of her.

"Iris is a linguist, a doctor of linguistics," I said. "She studies the way people talk."

"Like you?"

"Something like that. I teach about it, but I haven't done any research in years. Iris hasn't taught in years, but she can't seem to stop doing the research." I smiled in Iris' direction.

"Please," she said to Mama, "could you arrange a meeting with this Rachel Moon?"

"I can," I interrupted. "She homeschools Sissy during the school year, and I've met her."

Iris beamed and went back to eating all the sea morsels on her platter.

Iris paid the bill and waited outside with Pasquin while I had another word with Mama.

"When was Corwin in here last?"

"Just this morning, for breakfast. He showed up looking like he'd been all night on a shrimp boat. Had that brother of his with him. Both looked like they'd been swimming with the crabs."

"The brother, Aaron, who has been in jail in Jacksonville?"

"I don't know about that. Looked more like they'd both been out on the Gulf for days. Did a delivery last night and was headed to Moon Island." She didn't dwell on the meeting but changed the topic back to the cafe. "Do you have any idea what breakfast time smells like in this place when men who've been on a shrimp boat for days gather in here? Stinks worse than rancid oil."

Iris roared off in her car, shooting gravel up behind her.

"We just added about five years to that old darling's life," said Pasquin. "Did you see those eyes light up when she heard about Rachel?"

"That will be easy enough to arrange," I said, "provided Rachel is willing to be recorded. Of course, she'll have to talk about the legend of Oscar Moon."

"Let's go, woman. It's dark and your Vernon will be waiting. But!" He held up a finger. "Your trusty boat chauffeur is going to show you something and then take you home." Pasquin started the motor and guided the boat onto a dark river. The moon, covered by a cloud, gave no light to the creatures who would watch as he crept across the water.

We headed upriver, passing his landing and Edwin's and moving closer to some lights in the distance.

"There," he said. He pulled the boat under a tree on the opposite side of the river. Lights on tall poles shined on a newly constructed dock. One man in tall rubber boots, went about sweeping water over the loading area. There was no sign to designate it as a delivery area, but that would have been obvious to any fisherman. "Craw Fish Dock," he said. "Shrimp boats who sell around here come and unload right there. Not the ones owned by the big companies. They use the bay side docks." He pointed to a truck moving down a road and approaching the building. "There's a truck now. They'll unload the shrimp and cart them off to fill the bellies of diners."

Woods surrounded the building. The only light was either on the dock itself, coming from the vehicles down a lonely road or the moon itself.

CHAPTER THIRTEEN

The house was dark when I walked into the front yard. My presence triggered the sensor lights that lit up each side of the yard and the steps at the screen door. Vernon was nowhere in sight.

"Okay, Plato, why aren't you here to guard the place?" I looked and listened for the swamp dog but he made no appearance. The porch creaked just enough to stop the frogs from croaking beneath the boards on ground that never really dried. It harbored damp-loving creatures and tonight it was frogs. If something had run beneath the porch, hundreds of the green amphibians would hop about on their way to the river refuge. A water moccasin had once invited himself to house there, too, and for all I knew he was back again. I never worried much about anyone hiding there. A bed of frogs, slithery snakes, the occasional salamander and molding leaves are not exactly a haven for a thief or worse.

I stood near the screen door and looked about the porch. Nothing was hiding there. The front door was still locked. Inside, I flipped the switch as soon as I could and flooded the downstairs with light. The only thing I saw was a rolled piece of paper sticking above the rim of a decorative vase. A place where Pasquin and Vernon left notes if they had to be in the house for a reason.

Couldn't wait. We dive Moon Lake tomorrow. Be ready a.m. Vernon.

It was Saturday. when Law enforcement only worked on urgent cases.

Leaving a note like that meant Vernon wanted no calls. His cell phone would be turned off, and he wanted no messages on his home phone. Tony may be with him, and I wouldn't risk calling him. Instead, I went to the carport and got my diving gear ready for tomorrow. Clouds were moving fast in a light breeze, allowing the moon to shine again. I had checked the air in my tank and was securing it in the back of my Honda when I heard the boat in the distance.

Hurrying to my landing, I didn't stand on the deck but risked the water by climbing down the ladder. I waited in water up to my armpits. The shrimp boat came towards me, its lights casting eerie dots against the natural moon beams. It moved slowly, its pilot standing under a dim light. He looked out as he did the last time, his eyes searching my dock. When he opened a spotlight and shined it over the landing, I knew he was looking for me. I ducked beneath the surface. When the spotlight disappeared, I came up and heard the motor moving farther up the river. It wasn't going any faster, and the motor completely stopped in the distance. I never heard it start up again.

Deciding I was hearing, or not hearing, things, I climbed out of the water and headed to the house. In the carport, I pulled a towel from the car and dried off as much as possible. Inside, I stripped off the wet clothes, emptying the pockets of wet tissues and lip balm and an oyster knife.

"Oh, damn! I forgot to return this to Sissy," I said. I placed it on the table by the door, thought better of that, and stuck it in the drawer.

Sometime in the night, my head spinning with dreams of ghost ships floating in the currents, I heard Plato raise a fuss. I staggered downstairs to let him in. The front sensor lights had come on again, and there he was, covered in nasty river mud.

"Where have you been?" I said as I grabbed a handful of neck hair and pulled him to the hose outside the front steps. "It's not like you to crawl around in stuff like this." I pulled off some hydrilla grass sections that had entangled itself in his wiry coat. "You've been swimming, right? One of these days, dog, a gator is going to have you for a cocktail."

Plato wiggled and shook until I had him completely free of mud and was wiping him down with the towel. I stroked the cloth over his feet and when I went down his back leg, he yelped. There was blood on the towel.

"Where've you been?" Checking the wound, I found it more of a puncture that had stopped bleeding until I hit the scab with the towel. There was dark brown and bright red blood on it. I rubbed my hand through his wiry coat and hit a sharp piece of metal. It was the barb from barb wire, as though at had fallen off, maybe rusted off, and Plato had come across it in the mud. I pulled it from his fur and looked at it in the light. Old stuff, I thought.

"See what scrounging in the swamp does to you, old mutt?"

Inside, I applied anesthetic to the wound. It didn't impair his walking or seem to hurt him.

"You'd better eat something and get some rest. Sometime tomorrow, you may end up going to a vet."

Plato fell onto his pillow as soon as he finished the dog food and lapped up nearly a bowl of water. He had been busy, but then swamp dogs were like that. He wagged his tail a couple of times and dropped off to sleep.

I lay on the couch, hoping to drop off, too, but also to hear if anything came back down the river. By the time I retrieved a thin blanket, I was too sleepy to notice anything. I'd have to count on a sleeping dog to wake me if any odd sounds or scents came from outside locked doors.

The sun streamed through when I opened the curtain the next morning. I checked Plato's wound. It seemed okay but I reapplied antibiotic cream and let him out the door. He came back for food, but as soon as he finished I let him out again and down the path he went, running into the swamp.

A patrol car appeared from the other direction about the same time.

"Loman?" I didn't expect Tony's sergeant to be in a marked car.

"Sorry, Luanne. Tony called and got me out of bed. You're to head for Moon Lake in your own car. Bring your diving gear, and park on the road just before the bridge."

"Where are the Moons?" I asked.

"I don't know much, but they aren't to know about this. Had people watching the house. The old lady is still there, or at least she never came outside. The girl has gone off with the pothead, and the men left in a boat last night."

"Headed which way?"

Loman shrugged. "I wasn't on watch. You'll have to ask the others when you get there."

"Aren't you going, too?"

He shook his head. "I've got another assignment."

The patrol car backed down the road and around the bend. Something was different. Usually, they would have driven me in the car.

I pulled on the bathing suit and tossed on jeans and a tee-shirt over it. The Honda bounced over the ruts and roared as I gunned it to go the long way round to Moon Island.

Before I came to the makeshift bridge, I saw an unmarked car that I recognized as the one Vernon often used. I parked behind it and saw Tony step out of the woods.

"Bring your gear. Vernon is ready to go." He put his finger to his lips to remind me that the swamp had ears.

I followed him into the trees and came to a clearing where Vernon stood in a wet suit, mask and fins in hand. He was at one end of the clearing, looking through branches of low growing scrubs.

"Get dressed. We'll walk to the house side of the lake, where old Oscar was supposed to have gone in. Can't risk going in the swimming side. Teens have already shown up for a swim."

I struggled with the wet suit and joined Vernon at his lookout. Four teenage boys jumped off vines into deep water, just missing the sloping underwater bank. They had to be careful or one would end up with a broken neck. Vernon motioned for me to follow him in the other direction. We moved through trees and scrub until we stood beneath the oak at water's edge.

"What are we looking for?" I asked, "a body?"

He nodded, "Patel's."

"Why isn't the dive team doing this?"

"They're busy at sea." He gently placed a finger over my lips and shook his head. "Go quietly into the water and stay away from prying eyes," he whispered. We pulled on the tanks in the shadow of the branches. He gave a thumbs-up sign and turned toward the lake.

I shrugged and followed him into the water without a splash.

Vernon slid into the deep quietly and I did the same to keep the boys from seeing us. He motioned for me to swim above him.

I knew the routine. Check the debris and vegetation that lodged itself on the sink walls. He'd do the same a few feet below me. That way, we could search the banks and keep our eye out for each other.

The dark water surrounded us almost immediately but we waited until we were several feet down before turning on the mask lamps. The small light shined spots on the wall of the sinkhole, revealing a lot of oak tree branches that had fallen and caught on the sides. Some appeared to be growing out of the wall, but that was misleading. Nothing about it was alive. We moved around the wall, poking into thick branches and occasional other debris like a bag of empty beer cans. I tried to remember where that was. Sissy could use the money from recycling if we ever brought them to the surface. We moved slowly, trying not to break off loose dirt from the walls. Vernon's tank was visible below me as he stopped, searched, and moved on. I could feel the water getting colder as we went down. The sinkhole had an aquifer, a natural spring beneath it.

The sides held nothing that would indicate a body in the hole. One could be there but it might have drifted down, far deeper than any police diver would go. Vernon searched as close to the swimming area as he dared. We were deep below the swimmers but we could see their bare feet and legs in a rush of bubbles as they jumped in from the high bank. Here, he went deeper, motioned for me to do the same and we searched for signs—ripped clothing, pocket items, hair stuck on a branch—anything to let us know someone had been dumped here. When we came to a narrow bend that led even deeper and would have been treacherous to enter without removing the tanks, we turned back. By the time we reached the side where we began, the boys had gone.

"There's nothing here, Luanne." Vernon breathed heavily as he pulled himself onto the bank. "Can you make it?" When I said yes, he jerked off the fins and mask and headed into the trees.

"Nothing," said Vernon to Tony. "Unless he went down nude and kept going into the depths, he's never been there." He unzipped the wetsuit and stripped it to his waist.

"I have an idea," I said.

Tony and Vernon stopped and stared at me.

"What do you know about this?" Tony said, his eyes narrowing.

"Nothing, other than you think Patel is in the water. I know you don't want to tell me why he'd be there, but I figure it'll have to come out soon if you plan on keeping me on the job." I wrapped a towel around my wet hair. "Follow me back to my house."

Vernon and I stayed in the suits on the drive. His big unmarked car bumped along behind my Honda. I pulled into the carport, and Vernon moved his vehicle into the trees. It wouldn't be spotted by anyone unless he walked into it.

"Last night, a shrimp boat came up the river. It shined its light on the dock while I hid in the water. Now, I think it was the same pilot who waved at me the night before. Was he just being friendly to see if I was still there? Maybe? But, I could swear he stopped somewhere upriver. And there's the matter of the dog."

Tony smirked. "Don't tell me he didn't bark in the night."

"Well, he didn't. At least not that I could hear. He did come back covered in the worst muck I've seen yet. And, he had a wound on his hind leg."

"Is that unusual?"

"For Plato? Yes."

Vernon smiled with his head down. My reasoning was too vague for Tony. "So where do we look?"

"I'd say let's go around the bend, where a boat would be out of sight to anyone standing on the landing, and dive there."

"The current could be strong there."

"Could be, but there are cypress trees and lots of things growing off the banks. Entanglement would be easy."

Tony paced, his jaw working. "Doesn't make sense to dump him in the river when he could be tossed at sea."

"There'd be others on a shrimp boat," I said. "Unless they were all in a conspiracy with each other, someone might see it happen. At night, on a delivery, the other shrimpers would either be off the boat or asleep below."

Vernon glanced at Tony and stifled another smile. He looked back at me. "Get the canoe."

We loaded the tanks into the canoe with almost no room left for us. Tony would stay on the dock and swat mosquitoes.

"If Pasquin comes by, just tell him to bring you around the bend," I said.

We paddled around cypress knees and across long strings of river grass in my red canoe, a gift of love from Vernon a few years back. It had scratches now, and water had worn some of the red off the side. It's name, Peace Offering, still stood out in white. I'd seen to that, repainting it when it faded.

We slowed when we were out of sight of the dock. The spot could be on either side of the wide river and it may take some diving to cover all of it. There was also the terrible thought that if a body had been tossed in the shallows, an alligator may have already made a meal of it. I looked for deep spots where a body could be sunk with a weight, and for shadowed sections of water where a body could be hidden. It seemed impossible with the miles of river and endless areas to look. We had nearly given up and planned to call the dive team to look in the area. Plato saved the day.

In a spot where there used to be a small boat house and now only a few poles sticking about the water surface, we heard barks coming from the shore.

"That's Plato!" I said and guided the canoe in that direction.

Plato met us in the shallows, his barking loud and friendly, yet somehow frantic. He was again covered in mud.

"What is it?" I said and moved out of the canoe.

Vernon pulled it on shore and laid the paddles on top of the tanks. Plato had taken off at a run to the other side of the poles where water bubbled up from an aquifer. The shore here was muddy for several steps until it dropped off into deep water. Plato stood in short grass and a few inches of water. Digging frantically in the shore mud, he stuck his face into the wetness.

"He can't smell through the water, can he?" asked Vernon.

"I wouldn't think so, but this is a swamp dog. If the scent is strong enough, who knows? We can smell dead things in the water. Why can't a dog?"

"We need to go off the edge," he said. "I'll get the gear."

I checked the water. Pristine water was coming from the depths and it looked clear. Only at the edge did it mix with the swamp elements. Farther out, the grass just below the surface moved with the swift currents that headed our way. Maybe something could have been washed this way, I thought. Plato is smelling death.

We helped each other with the tanks and pulled on the fins. Vernon had his mask lowered when I took a last look at Plato. The dog had stopped digging. He wasn't barking, but whining from his throat. In his mouth, he held the short rounded handle of an oyster shucking knife.

CHAPTER FOURTEEN

Plato had sense enough to grab the wooden end of the knife. The short, flat and very sharp end stuck out the other side of his mouth.

"That's what he was digging up," I said. I moved closer to the edge. He had been digging where the water was an inch or so deeper from where we stood.

"It could have washed up here," said Vernon. He gently held Plato's head and took the knife from his mouth. He paused to give him praise and an ear rub. "We'll have to stick it beneath an oar for now."

"What's that?" I pointed to some wire poking out of the mud.

Vernon moved closer. He picked up a stick and placed it under the wire. When he pulled it from the mud, he gave a short curse.

"Looks like someone has been tossing debris around here. This is an old piece of barbed wire. Not a nice thing to step on."

"Bag it," I said. "Plato has a wound from a barb."

"Whatever you say, sergeant." Vernon smiled and placed it in the canoe with the knife.

"Wait here," I said to Plato, knowing that was like telling a leaf not to blow in the wind. I appealed to his sense of ownership and pointed for him to sit inside the canoe. He obeyed, at least for the moment.

Vernon and I slipped into the water, finding ourselves in several feet almost immediately. A ship's pilot would know this, that an aquifer existed here, that there was no danger of running aground just at this point. A pilot and a body dumper.

The currents were here, too, and they pushed against us, aiming us back toward the bank. Would the pilot know that as well? Swimming against the current we moved into the darkness of the river. We traveled a short distance when we turned around and searched the sloping bottom and underwater banks for anything that would have drifted toward the point where Plato found the knife.

It didn't take long. Against the bank at a curve where broken limb debris had been caught a hand waved toward us, beckoning like Captain Ahab. It was a naked man caught on submerged tree limbs. If we hadn't been looking for Patel we would have easily missed him. His body would have drifted farther down and away, maybe resting in the depths for years until a drought uncovered bones.

I shined my mask light in the direction of where the face should be. The head tilted back, the thick black hair caught in the debris. Washed clear by the cold water, the neck gaped with a hole, a wound in the carotid area. If he hadn't bled to death before he hit water, he surely did here, and the blood had been washed away, mixing with pure aquifer water, dead leaves, and bank dirt.

Vernon gave the motion to surface. We hadn't brought much equipment with us but there was a float in the canoe. He marked the site while I phoned Tony, who was still standing on my landing. I gave him directions, through mud, leaves and tangled brush, but pretty much a straight line. It would take long minutes and colorful words for him to reach us.

Plato seemed to know he was the hero. He stuck around, allowing members of the dive team and other deputies to rub his ears and tell him what a smart dog he was. Vernon and I had to pull the canoe well into the trees to make room for the scene people to collect whatever evidence they could find.

Patel's body was finally removed from its watery niche to the bank. A rusted strand of barbed wire encircled one ankle. Marshall Long, the scene tech, spread his large thighs and knelt in the mud to give it the once over before hauling it to the lab table.

"Quick, efficient jab into the artery with the oyster knife. It's not long but doesn't have to be in this case. If he couldn't stop the bleeding right away, he'd die." He dropped the knife into an evidence bag, handed it off to an assistant, and spread his arms—his signal to the deputies to help him stand. The hem of his white coat, soaked and muddy, attached itself to his pants legs. He never wore socks with his runners. The shoes made a sucking sound as he pulled them out of the mud.

"What's with the barbed wire?" asked Tony.

"It's old and brittle, but I'll bet somebody rigged a weight to try to hold the body on the bottom of the river. Look at the scratches on that leg. It may have been placed higher up but didn't hold and moved to the ankle. The weight dropped off. You might find it out there." Marshall smiled in my direction. "Divers have all the fun." He grunted and moved to drier ground. "None of this is official, you know. Just speculation." He moved to some grass and began scraping mud off his shoes.

Vernon and I finally made it back to my place to change clothes. We'd meet Tony at the department to give our statements, and, I hoped, someone would explain to me why one of Sissy's borders had been sent away, permanently.

Tony paced the floor of his office, ready to snap at anything that got in his way. A couple of folders did, and he kicked them to the other side where their papers spilled onto the floor. A deputy knelt and tried to sort them back into their proper places.

"How the hell did this happen?" said Tony angrily. "We pay an informant and let him get slaughtered?"

"I don't think we had that intention," said Loman, his sleepy eyes wide open now. He swiped a handkerchief across his face. "He must have taken a chance, got caught snooping."

"Tell us what you saw those two nights," Tony nearly screamed at me.

"Now, just a minute. I had no idea you guys had paid anyone to do anything. Find someone else to yell at."

Tony glanced at Vernon who glared back.

"Okay, okay," Tony said and calmed himself to the point of restating his question. "What exactly happened with those shrimp boats you saw?"

"They may have been the same boat. I wouldn't swear to it, but I think they were." I went on to describe the first night with the pilot waving and the second with the spotlight. I took a deep breath when I finished, and asked, "Now, what are you looking for that you needed an informant?"

Tony finally sat down after tossing a box from his chair.

"It's not just us. In fact, it's mostly the Feds, including the Coast Guard. They asked us for help, because they think some of this may be starting miles away from the Gulf and moving this way."

"What's happening?"

He looked at Vernon and nodded for him to tell me. It was always like that. He hired me to do jobs for the department but anything sensitive went to Vernon.

"The Feds think illegal aliens are getting through by working on boats. There's no checking of credentials in these boat jobs. Just hire on experienced shrimpers and let them sleep aboard a few nights, then lay them off. They go on to another job."

I nodded. "Go on to another job—like shucking oysters?"

"Could be. Even harvesting and selling them. They'd work for the small houses that didn't have Workmen's Comp. As long as they could show they knew how to shuck..."

"Sanchez!" Tony stood up and shoved his chair into a wall. "We think he ran because he thought someone was checking on the place."

I closed my eyes, a cold realization passing through me. "I caused that."

"You?"

"I remember someone saying I was the woman who helped the cops on cases. That's when Sanchez acted as though he would choke and took off across the dock. He fell and died because he thought I was there to arrest him."

The office, full of deputies in both uniform and plain clothes, stood silent.

"The women, the Hispanic women, eventually ran, too," said Tony. "You said they helped pull the guy out, but they didn't stick around. Now, no one can locate them."

"Someone moved Patel's things from his room on Moon Island," I said.

"How do you know that?" said Tony. He made a quick glance at Vernon, but I wasn't going to let him take flack.

"Sissy told me. Said he just left and took his clothes. But, he left his bathroom things, which I find a bit bothersome. I mean if I'm going to leave, I'd take my comb and toothbrush."

"Yeah." Tony stared down at his desk for a moment. "I have to call the Feds, but I'm going to try and get a search warrant for that house and maybe the entire island." He raised his head. "And all of you keep quiet about this, even to that little girl."

"Finding a body in the river is going to get out, Tony. Too many people saw the scene guys at work." I didn't relish trying to keep this from swamp people.

"We don't have to say he was murdered, just that he drowned. We may have blown the operation already, but keep it under your hat until I have a chance to sort things with the Feds."

We walked toward the elevators but were stopped when Tony called out, "On second thought, don't say anything about the guy being Indian. We'll tell the press we haven't identified him yet."

"So what do we do now?" I said as Vernon and I stood in the parking lot.

"Best thing is for you to stay aware of what's around you. I don't know who dumped this guy overboard, but he knows you stand on that dock sometimes. I don't want you being the target of a skittish killer."

"Somehow, Vernon, neither do I. Then, again, I'm kind of scared for Sissy. She goes up and down that river by herself all the time."

He nodded. "We'll be patrolling, of course. Only we won't be doing it in a marked boat. Just keep that old dog close by." He squeezed my arm, about the only affection I'd get while we were working. They all knew about our relationship, but we had to be discreet.

"I'm off to Fogarty Spring," I said. "I need to make arrangements for Iris to interview Rachel Moon."

"Be there long?" He smiled and looked at the sky.

"Certainly not all night."

"I'll stop at Mama's Table and bring crab cakes."

With the promise of an evening together, I stepped lightly

into my Honda and drove the long road to the little town named after my ancestors. Nothing much was left of them except the name and my swamp house, and it wasn't even in the town. The history was kept in a little library branch, nothing more than a one room structure with a good roof.

On the way, I met trucks carrying heavy equipment that had been raking out swamps, draining them and building foundations for stilted houses that would cost more money than Sissy ever imagined there was in the world. Those houses would soon dot the waterline across from her island and be populated with people educated in big brick schools and retired on high return stocks. How long before Sissy's own island was divided into lots? Another place in danger of makeover was the waterline at Fogarty Spring. Rachel Moon's pretty little cottage would bring a good price.

"Rachel?" I said when the woman opened the door. Her hair fell in disarray about her shoulders. She wore a dingy robe.

"Sorry," she said. "I was napping."

From the reek, I figured out what she did to put herself to sleep. I hadn't pictured her as a drinker, and this took me by surprise.

"I've come to ask a favor for a colleague," I said.

After a few moments of blinking hard, she moved aside and held the door open for me. Inside, the place was stifling with the humidity and shut windows. I didn't feel air conditioning anywhere and wondered how she lived in this.

"Let me splash my face, okay?"

I nodded and watched her shuffle down the hall. From my chair, I looked about the room, still convinced it was the typical country school teacher's abode. Until I saw the book on a side table. It was a academic treatise on the repeated instances of child abuse in family situations. I had figured Rachel for a romance novel reader, or at least someone who would read Agatha Christie. The book appeared to be filled with actual cases and lots of psychiatric jargon. On a whim, I turned to the index and looked up Moon. I sighed with relief when I didn't find it there.

"Now, what kind of favor are you asking for?" She had dampened her hair and pushed it behind her ears.

"I have an elderly colleague, a retired linguistics professor, who is doing a dialect study. It would seem it's more for fun than for publication, but she's already recorded Beatrice Moon, and she'd like to record you. I think she plans to do the same with Sissy when everyone finds the time."

"Well, what about Corwin and his brother—if you can find them."

"Yes, but we haven't asked either of them yet. And Aaron is back at the Moon house."

Rachel opened her eyes wide and placed a hand over her mouth. I couldn't tell if she was stifling a burp or surprised at the arrival of her other cousin.

"He was in jail, I heard." She kept the hand over her mouth and stared at me.

I shrugged. "I don't know the details, but if he was in jail, he's out now."

"What does this entail with your professor?"

"She'll ask you to talk on a subject and record you. She's not looking for a true story or anything. It's just if you all talk on the same subject, you're likely to use the same vocabulary. She can compare and come to a conclusion about patterns."

"And she enjoys that?"

"Immensely."

"Nothing I would like less than sit and listen to somebody tell stories over and over." She stopped and removed her hand. "I suppose she then has to go and listen again when she compares them. How boring!"

"No, it's not boring. She knows what to listen for and will have those patterns down in no time. It seems you Moons have a way of talking, making your own past tense with some words, that's unique."

"A Moon dialect?" She picked up an empty glass near her book. "Would you like something... lemonade, perhaps?"

I sat in the stifling room and drank two glasses of lemonade. Outside, the sun was setting and I had Vernon waiting at my house to feed me crab cakes and sweet nothings. Rachel had picked the moment to keep talking. Her lemonade looked a little less yellow than mine, closer to the amber of a good rum.

"That little Sissy is a pretentious brat at times," she said. "I've had to correct her more than once about telling stories about her great grandma to other little kids. Makes the woman out to be a witch and laughs when she scares them." She sipped from her glass and leaned over to tap my hand. "Mind you, she was a witch, or like one, at times. Takened—took—a switch to me once when I was in my teens. Much too old to be whipped."

"What had you done?"

"Paraded around in my bathing suit, she said! Imagine that. She thought I should at least wear a terry robe from the house to the lake. Said all the boys were watching me." She smiled in triumph. "I knew that, of course. They even sat on the docked boats and stared at me." She tossed her head like a small girl. "Not a one of them complained."

CHAPTER FIFTEEN

I left Rachel Moon's little house as soon as she agreed to let Iris see her. She was beginning to nod off from her "lemonade." It was after dark and Vernon would be waiting, but the bouncy ride over dirt roads went for nothing. He wasn't there, and there was no message. That meant a phone blackout for a while.

Instead of a cuddly night with crab cakes and Vernon, I picked up the phone and let Iris know she should call Rachel and make arrangements to record her. The professor's voice was ecstatic, promising me a huge dinner to celebrate when she had enough for a preliminary paper.

"Do you plan to publish?" I asked.

"You never know. I've done enough of it in my time, and another little article for a journal would tickle me to no end."

"You'll want to record Sissy, too, right?"

"Oh, my yes. The fact that a dialect has been passed on to children who, as you know, speak the language of their peers, is quite a find."

"Will you do this soon?"

"Tomorrow, my dear doctor."

I hung up wondering if Rachel would drink herself into a stupor and not remember that she had made a promise. Maybe when

Iris identified herself as a professor, it would trigger something in Rachel's ego.

The next call went to Pasquin.

"You've been busy I hear," he said when he picked up his phone. Laughter burst out in the background. "Tulia and Edwin are here. I made up some fish stew and they're seeing who can get it down without something cold and wet."

It would be hot stuff. Even at his age, Pasquin wanted his food to burn the tongue like it did in his youth when the old Cajun dishes came with peppery red sauce.

"What have you heard about my being busy?"

"Finding a body in the river. Didn't have on any clothes. That sort of stuff."

"Pasquin," I sighed. The swamp has eyes and ears that not even cops can evade. "Have you heard anything else. Tell me."

"Man was Patel from the Moon house boarders. Got a knife in the neck. Your swamp hound found the weapon. That enough?"

"How?"

"Just heard. You know, from the swamp vines."

"Can the swamp vines keep it quiet from the outside, especially the papers?"

"Now, ma'am, you know exactly the answer to that. It may bounce off the cypress knees but it's like the sound of a deep underground river. Nobody above can interpret that."

"And watch your back. We don't know who did this yet."

"Your hound," he said and turned away from the phone for a moment, "he's here in case you're looking for him."

"Plato will sit anywhere if he's fed. Are you giving him stuff with hot sauce?"

"Old dog won't have it. He's gnawing a steak bone."

"Do me a favor tomorrow. Take him to the vet in Fogarty Spring and get that little wound on his back leg looked at. He got it from rusty barbed wire. Tell the vet to put it on my bill."

I left the old guy with his party of swamp people and one hero dog. He was having more fun than I was. I stared at a folder of papers on a side table. I had meant to have them back to the students by now. Giving up, I grabbed the folder, a red pen, and started the routine. Somewhere after the fifteenth deep structure diagram, my mind drifted, wondering about Sissy and how much education she got from Rachel. The kid would be world weary once in her teens. That big house with only a demented old woman and men in it, what would it mean to a teenage girl? It couldn't be safe, and I knew I would have to suggest something. It would have to be indirect, maybe subtle, but she shouldn't be there under those conditions. Maybe she could become a guide for Iris. The professor would need more recordings to see if the patterns repeated themselves or if they were only from a one family dialect. I resisted the idea of taking her in here.

Knocking off the last of the papers, I tossed the folder on a table and stretched out on the floor. My back had just about removed its kinks when the phone rang.

"Miz Fogarty," a female voice spoke to me, "this is Sergeant Kelly at the sheriff's office. Vernon Drake asked me to relay this information to you: Aaron Moon was never in jail in Jacksonville or the surrounding areas. In fact, we aren't sure where he was for the past four months."

I thanked her and moved to the porch. The darkness and sounds of live critters in the swamps cleared my mind. Sissy and her great-grandmother believed Aaron was in jail. But, he hadn't been. Hence the need for a search warrant.

Sunday morning brought a bell from the river that I hadn't

heard before, a clang that rousted me from bed. Pulling on some jeans and a tee-shirt, I ran to the landing. My eyes didn't believe what I was seeing—a floating church. The boat was a converted tourist job with open windows and a cover for rain. It might hold sixty people in a pinch. Someone had written "Jesus Saves" across the side and perched a church bell on top. It rocked back and forth, clanging for river residents to get up and see God. Or, actually hear Him. That wouldn't be a problem. The reverend at one end was using a microphone.

I shook my head as the boat moved at a slow drift. A few people sat on board and waved at me as they passed. One shouted if I'd like to join them. I shook my head as they yelled blessings for the day. The preacher continued to belt out his sin and damnation, aiming at the party goers of the night. He was out of range for the rich folk. They were closer to the Gulf in the big houses. Pasquin and his hot stew and bourbon party would get an earfull.

"Evangelicals gone wild," I said and headed back to the house. Before I reached the steps, I heard Plato bark down the river. He would be after the noisy boat, shooing them away from disturbing our universe. I sat on the top step and waited for him.

"Want to take a trip to Moon Island?" I asked Plato after he'd had his breakfast. He wagged his tail and plopped on his pillow. "Evidently not. Why would you when you've been partying all night?" Obviously, he hadn't seen the vet. Pasquin was most likely still asleep.

Moon Island came to me. Sissy showed up, causing Plato to bark without moving much but his head.

"Go back to sleep, puppy dog. She's not the one you need to watch."

"I came to have a swimming lesson if you've got time," she

said. "You promised." She held up a bathing suit. "I borrowed it from a friend in Fogarty Spring." I didn't remember making such a promise, but I could have. In spite of her great-grandma's prudishness, I knew she needed to know how to swim.

"Have you been to see Rachel this morning?" I held the door for her to enter. Giving her a swimming lesson sounded like something I needed at the moment.

"Yeah. She didn't feel good, but I had to ask her for the address of one of my classmates who said I could borrow her suit."

"Her parents didn't mind?"

Sissy shook her head and smiled. "They were too busy getting all the other kids ready for Sunday School."

Who needs to get ready? I asked myself. Now you can walk out to the water's edge and listen in your pajamas.

"Have you eaten anything?"

She shook her head. "I thought you weren't supposed to eat before going into the water."

"A big meal, no, but you can't swim around in that cold stuff on an empty stomach." I took her into the kitchen and gave her some toast with hot tea and milk. "Try a sausage, just one," I said and handed her one on a fork.

"Who makes breakfast at your place?" I knew the answer but I wanted it confirmed.

"I make it for myself and Grandma when Uncle Aaron isn't there. He likes to cook up big meals when he comes. When I left, he was just cracking some eggs and frying oysters on the side."

"Eggs and oysters for breakfast?"

"Coffee, too, and I think he brought some oranges."

"Sissy," I leaned over to pour some more warm tea in her cup. "When did Aaron get out of jail?"

She looked at me and shrugged. "He didn't say, but he had

enough time to get home and to bring those oranges."

"He came back by himself?"

"Most likely got a bus or hitched a ride to Tallahassee."

"And Corwin picked him up there?"

She nodded. "Can I put on the suit now?"

We both changed into suits, grabbed towels and headed for the shore near the landing.

"You have to watch for snakes and gators in swamp waters," I said. "Gators especially like small kids," I joked and splashed cold water on her, all the while glancing into the bushes to make sure no reptile waited for Moon food.

Sissy took to being in the water about the same way she did being on top of it. She was a natural. Her first inclination like any kid was to dog paddle, but when I showed her how to float and move her arms gently, she had no trouble staying above the water. The fun part was holding her breath and sitting in the clear area. She practiced it over and over, asking me to time her.

"You can swim underwater, you know. You have to do that if you ever want to dive with a scuba tank."

From that moment, her little skinny body practiced hand and arm movements and frog kicking along with holding her breath and keeping her eyes open in the water.

"Can I use one of your face masks?"

"Only when I know you can swim without any help, face mask included," I said.

The lesson came to a halt when Plato appeared on the dock. I had left the door ajar so he could get out after his sleep. When he saw us, he dashed to the landing, watched Sissy for a moment, and jumped into the water with her. I tossed her a swimming tube, and the two of them played chase. I sat on the dock and watched for predators. The question of who would watch for grown predators on Moon Island nagged at me. I had no answer.

My mind drifted to Moon Lake years ago. Rachel, a budding teen, would appear alone at the side and drop her towel. Men on tied-up boats would watch silently. Maybe there were some boys in the trees, too. The lake would have been empty of people. Mermaid Rachel would have it all to herself. I could see her leave the towel on the shore and stand for a moment in the sunlight, displaying the firm body of youth, her long hair flowing around her shoulders. She'd pull it up and wrap it in a ribbon right there on shore where all could see. Once she'd done with her bathing suit show, she'd dive off into the sinkhole depths, rising on the other side, and walk onshore. Her suit and body and hair would be wet, caressing her just like the men's eyes. "Gavi said so," I told myself. "Was Beatrice Moon watching, too?"

"Are you expected back on Moon Island for lunch?" I had to yell over the barking and laughing.

"I'm supposed to buy Grandma a hamburger," she said. "But that means going back to Fogarty Spring."

"Tell you what. You get dressed and take the boat back to the island. I'll take the car, stop for burgers for all of us, and you can meet me at the bridge and help carry them back."

She smiled and raised herself onto the tube.

"How many people do I need to buy for?"

"Not sure. Corwin and Trukee were gone early to get on a shrimp boat. Uncle Aaron said he'd have to be off soon, but he was still there when I left."

"I'll get extras, just in case."

Sissy left the suit in my guest bath. She said her friend told her it was an old one and she could use it all summer. "At least she's got a friend her age," I said under my breath.

Plato showed no inclination to get in either the boat or the car.

Instead, he trotted off down the lane toward Pasquin's house. Maybe now he'd get to the vet.

I pulled into the fast food drive-thru on the highway just out of Fogarty Spring and headed for the island. I parked in the spot near the rickety bridge, trying to camouflage the car in the bushes. The water came up to my soles when I walked across the old boards. Sissy stood on the other side.

"Nobody's here but Grandma right now, and she's napping. She always does that when Uncle Aaron comes because he makes big old breakfasts and it puts her right to sleep."

"Shouldn't she be awake by now?" I wondered if Uncle Aaron may have included a sleeping pill with the oysters.

"Should, but she's not. I'll take her food up and sit with her while she eats it." She took one of the bags.

"There's enough for five people," I said. "Don't know how cold meat and fries will taste later."

She grinned, her eyes wide with glee. "But now we can microwave them! Uncle Aaron brought one with him."

"From jail?" It slipped out, not something I wanted to remind a kid about, but she didn't seem to care.

"He got it on the way here."

A house with no phone line and no television, but a microwave. The Moons had their modern improvements a little confused.

"Better not zap the fries. You could cause a grease fire."

We trudged up the stairs and entered Beatrice's room. The old woman pushed herself up when she heard us and stared blankly for a moment.

"You wanted a hamburger, Grandma," said Sissy and held one up in its orange wrapper.

The woman grinned and held out her hand. Sissy gave it to her and immediately pulled a folded cloth from a chair and spread it over the woman's legs up to her waist. She sat down and took a burger for herself. "You want to eat with us or maybe downstairs?"

I got the message. Watching Grandma eat in bed wasn't something she wanted me to do. I nodded and turned to the window. Pushing aside the curtain, I looked down at the lake. There was the big oak, its branches nearly touching the surface where Oscar was said to have gone into the water. Was Beatrice watching from this spot? If so, she would see him only when he reached the edge. Or, perhaps the oak limbs weren't as low and full as they are now. After all, it was 1959. But these old trees would have been close to this size back then, their limbs healthy and full near the water. Oscar emerged from beneath the tree limbs and hit the water. Was that what she saw?

"I'll eat on the porch, I think." The other burgers waited on the kitchen counter beside the brand new microwave. It wasn't an expensive one but would make a big difference for guests who had to make their own food. I took a burger and stood at the back door. It had a large pane of glass poorly installed. I looked out back. The lake was clear. I could see the oak better, and anything beneath the limbs might have been more visible. Perhaps I could have seen most of Oscar as he headed for the water. Maybe not his face, but certainly his arms and legs.

I wandered on to the front porch and rocked until I finished the fries. The sodas were in the refrigerator. I stood once again in the kitchen, sipping from a straw, and taking in all the things on the open shelves—open because the cabinet doors no longer shut properly. Spices, cardamom and coriander, that must have been owned by Patel lined the front of one shelf. I made a mental note to tell Vernon.

Inside the trash can was a plastic bag lining and the morning's breakfast papers tossed in—sausage packages, egg shells, a tube that held biscuit dough. Aaron knew how to eat. On the back of the counter near the door was a line of pill bottles. I picked them up. Mostly were over the counter pain relievers and cold medicines. There were a couple of prescriptions for sleeping pills and tranquilizers for Beatrice. Did she need to be kept calm?

Sissy came downstairs to get sodas for herself and Mrs. Moon. "Once she drinks this stuff, she'll be wide awake," she said. "She can't handle much caffeine and Uncle Aaron won't let her have it when he cooks breakfast."

"Your Uncle Aaron seems pretty efficient," I said. "Kind of him to cook breakfast."

I turned to look at Sissy walk to the stairs with two cans of cola. "Is he a good uncle?"

Sissy shrugged. "I guess so."

CHAPTER SIXTEEN

"Maybe the old lady has to be drugged at times," said Vernon. "And Patel's spices weren't moved. Did anyone question that when they thought he'd gone away?"

"No one complained to me, but only Sissy would have. Corwin and Trukee don't say much to me."

"I can't even try to figure it out now. I need a place to crash for a few hours, and I don't want to drive all the way home." He closed his eyes but smiled. He'd been sitting in a boat hidden between cypress knees and tall grass all night, on stakeout.

"We saw two shrimp boats go up the river. Our boats tailed them until they unloaded at the dock. Both turned around and went back towards the bay. Feds don't have enough manpower. They asked us to help out as long as we're in our own county."

And that was why he didn't show up with the crab cakes and seduction.

"Now, can I use your bed?" He opened his eyes and grinned, "Alone, of course."

"The bed, yes, but not necessarily alone," I said. "There's some salve for the mosquito bites in the medicine cabinet."

Joining him wasn't the wisest thing. I had classes to teach and coffee to drink before heading to campus. Life got in the way of relationships, but sometimes relationships are life. After he showered, I rubbed the mosquito salve on Vernon's bites. Our embraces weren't fast and furious like the last time, but urgent.

It was a typical Monday morning. Students were running late, dripping coffee cups, and wearing rumpled clothes from not doing the laundry over the weekend. I tried to keep it light by having volunteers make some of the guttural phonetic sounds not found in English. I looked away from the punchy group and saw Iris' smiling face peering through the rectangle window in the door. She made hand signals for me to meet her in my office.

"I'm going to Fogarty Spring today, recorder in hand! Seems Miz Rachel is in the mood to talk."

We made arrangements to meet at Mama's Table where she insisted on treating me again to what she called "such marvelous sea creatures."

"Did you get much out of the recordings of Mrs. Moon?"

"Oh, my yes. The woman talked and talked. She nodded off a couple of times, too, but I just waited for about five minutes and she was back at it again. I have much to analyze."

"I wonder if I might listen to some of it," I said. "I have no intention of using any of it to write a paper. Just curious to what she has to say about the incident of her husband's dropping himself into the lake."

"And what a mystery. The man must have just got tired of living—or he was drunk as a skunk!" She laughed at her cliché. "I tell you what, I'll burn a disk—as the youngsters say. I have learned to do that on my computer."

I waved good-bye to Iris as she headed for the parking lot. Her enthusiasm made me wonder if she had ever grown tired of doing the same lectures year after year, up against the same foibles of college freshmen. Perhaps it was the grad students that kept her sane.

I warned her that Rachel was an educated woman and might consciously avoid using the dialect. That was when Iris smiled and said she was taking along a nice bottle and would offer a nipper to make her talk.

"Will that invalidate your sample?" I asked.

She laughed, shaking her head, but not answering me.

Just as my last class of the day ended, Vernon called.

"Thanks for the bed. I slept like a rotten log most of the day. By the way, you need to hit a grocery store. And something else. The Feds aren't getting a search warrant for the Moon house. They say they don't have enough to do that, even though Patel lived there. He left, and there's no suspicion, or not enough, that anyone there killed him. They want to rely on stakeouts, maybe catch Corwin in smuggling humans and then do the search. Guess where that leaves me tonight, and possibly a lot more nights?"

"What if they need you on the dive team?"

"Then they'll pull me off stakeout duty. Look, Pasquin called and left you a message that he would eat at Mama's tonight. He wants to know if you'll join him. I told him if you wouldn't, I would."

We agreed to meet there. Iris would have to be bothered with their company, and knowing her, it wouldn't be any bother at all. How did such a social animal end up alone?

Vernon had to be on watch by nine o'clock. He couldn't tell the others that, only that he had a night shift. We met at six at Mama's Table. Iris wasn't there at first. I sat with Pasquin and Vernon, sipping iced tea, when she walked in the door with Rachel tagging along.

"I convinced her she'd be welcome and safe," she said and waited for Pasquin to pull up two chairs. Rachel took the one next to me, leaving the vacant one on her other side for Iris.

"Did you get your work done?" I asked.

"She talked me to death!" said Iris who ran a finger over the laminated menu. "And I appreciate every word." She reached a hand over and squeezed Rachel's wrist.

"Order for me, please," said Rachel in a small voice. "I'm not a regular in this place." Her eyes darted around the room, a place filling with fishermen tired of the long haul on water and ready for food and beer. Many grew up here and knew nothing but the fishing industry. Rachel probably had some old classmates among them.

"The platter is good," I said and nodded to Mama who kept an eye on Rachel. When she left us with all the orders, she rolled her eyes.

"I never really liked coming to this place," Rachel finally said. "The clientele tends toward ruffians."

"More like scruffians, if you ask me," said Pasquin. "These fellows make their living on the water. Don't have much time to wash up and iron their britches." He winked. He loved ribbing people like Rachel.

"And their language is crude," she said, unaware of Pasquin's teasing. "Now, Iris, if you want dialects, just record some of these characters. Nothing in their backgrounds told them how to speak in refined company."

"There probably is a fisherman's jargon, and maybe even one specific to this area. But an isolated family is more interesting to me." She leaned toward me. "I'm going to burn her disk for you, too. Maybe you can offer some ideas, hear patterns that I don't."

I nodded. Comparing her story with Beatrice's should be interesting, too.

One of Rachel's so-called characters had been staring at us since we sat down. He finally stood and approached our table, his mouth in a wide grin that emphasized a few day's stubble. He wore faded jeans and a matching jacket, the kind with lots of pockets.

"Miss Moon? Miss Rachel Moon?" He half bowed, held out a rough hand but jerked it back as though he didn't know how proper it was to shake someone's hand at the table.

Rachel raised one hand to her throat and looked from side to side. I wanted to say that it was okay, she was well protected. She nodded at the man.

"I thought so!" He broke into a laugh. "You don't remember little Henry Johnson, do you? You were my third grade teacher."

"Oh, my goodness," she said and blushed. "I don't often get remembered. My students were so young." She nodded and smiled at him.

"I own my own shrimp boat now. Doing pretty good out there on the water." He looked down at his clothes and ran a hand across his unshaven face. "It's not a job where you get to look like an executive, but it's good and free."

"You've done well for yourself, Henry. It's nice to know that people, at least some people, choose to do exactly what they want to do." She tilted her head and gave a half nod, clearly a dismissal.

"It's good to see you looking well," he said. "Better go back to my table. Food here is worth traveling upriver for, don't you agree?"

"I suppose," Rachel said and looked at her filled plate. She sounded like a school teacher now trying to elevate herself from the riff-raff.

"Well, good luck to you, ma'am," he nodded to the rest of us. "Enjoy your supper."

"Now, Rachel, that was lovely," said Iris. "If I hadn't dragged you here, you never would have seen that young man."

Rachel gave a nervous half smile. "Pity. I do hope that some of my little ones made it through college."

"Maybe he did," said Pasquin. "I met more than one fisherman who had a degree but couldn't stand working in an office. Maybe he prefers the wide open sea."

"I can't imagine," she said. "Why would he prefer to go around looking like that?"

"Looks about like the rest of folks in this place," Pasquin said.

Vernon winked at me. Like me, he knew the man most likely never made it out of high school, but Pasquin wasn't going to let Rachel get away with a put-down.

"Where did you go to college?" I asked Rachel.

"Oh, right where you teach," she said. "My parents lived in Carabelle, which was too far to commute every day. They put me up in a boarding house near school during the week, but drove up to get me every weekend."

"An all-girl boarding house?" Iris half smiled.

"My, yes. They never would have allowed me to stay in a mixed house, not even a dormitory."

We remained quiet for a moment, wondering what life had been like for this sheltered woman. I did the math in my head. College could have been an exciting time for her generation, at least a time when she might meet a future husband on the weekend. But Rachel went home with Mommy and Daddy every single weekend.

"And you taught in Carabelle, too?" I asked.

She nodded. "For years, and lived at home. I managed to save a lot."

"More than money, I'd imagine," said Pasquin and rolled his

eyes. I shot him a warning glance.

Rachel didn't notice his comment but rambled on and on about the kinds of children she had in her classes.

"Some had much promise," she said. "And I hope I had something to do with steering them right."

"I'm sure you did," said Iris and patted the woman's hand.

"When did you move to Fogarty Spring?" Vernon asked.

"That was quite a decision. You see, my father died and there were two women alone in a big house. I'd heard about the new elementary school opening here and asked for a transfer. We sold the old house and bought the little one I live in now. My mother lived in that house until the day she died." She smiled, proud of doing her duty, and stabbed a shrimp with her fork.

"It is a lovely place," said Iris. The woman was beginning to get on my nerves. She seemed to be ingratiating herself with her subject.

"You should come here more often," said Pasquin. "Get reacquainted with your kiddies." He held up his fork and pointed toward a large table where several seamen had ordered beer and fried platters. He could be sarcastic if he thought you were acting better than everyone around you.

I looked at Vernon and shook my head, trying to dart my eyes toward Pasquin. Someone needed to shut him up. Rachel wasn't the type to dance around the old man's sarcasm. In a moment, he'd be asking why she never married.

"How did the Moon children on the island get to school?" asked Vernon.

"By boat, I think," Rachel said. She said no more.

"How much fun that must have been," said Iris. "Imagine! Getting up in the morning, getting on a boat, and going down the river to school. That sounds like such an adventure for a child."

"The schools had rough boys," Rachel said. She nodded toward the table of men who laughed with abandon at some fish joke. "That's why I decided to take up home schooling for Sissy and some other young girls. They need a few graces."

Pasquin couldn't hold it in and gave a laugh. "I can see it now. Sissy serving tea and cakes to her old dad, the boarders, and the dainty Miz Beatrice."

"Anyone need more iced tea?" said Iris. She picked up the pitcher and offered to pour. Perhaps this gesture was to change the subject, but I decided she was saving Rachel's dignity.

Vernon looked at his watch and took a long drink from his filled glass. "I'm going to order a large one of these to go and then I'm off to work. Can't stand the coffee they brew in the office."

"Such a pity you have to work at night," said Iris. "But I'd guess you get more of the adventurous work at night, the time when most dirty deeds occur."

"Yes," I added. If only she knew that he would be sitting in a boat amongst cattail reeds and waiting for an occasional shrimp boat to pass by, only to relay the word to the next stakeout.

Vernon stared at her for a moment. "It happens," he said.

"I'll walk the ladies to their cars when we finish here," said Pasquin. He turned to Rachel, "and to the house."

We stayed after Vernon left. Iris insisted on trying the lemon pie and raved that it was worth every calorie. By the time we were ready to go, the place was full and others waited outside for a table.

"I'd really like to leave," said Rachel. "We can have coffee at my house."

"Coffee?" said Pasquin. "I thought you'd be more inclined to offer an after-repast liqueur." He stressed the last word and I scowled at him.

"Oh yes. I have a lovely one. Let's do go." Rachel was nervous. Rowdy men, perhaps, but she must be used to these people. When we moved outside and through the crowd of men, I realized why she didn't want to hang around. Coming from the dockside, Corwin and Aaron joined some other fishermen. She pretended not to see them, but I caught Corwin's eye. He nodded toward me and stared after his cousin.

Rachel seated us in her tiny living room and placed paper doilies on the tables near our chairs. When she brought out the tiny liqueur glasses, she made an effort to explain how they came from an antique store in Tallahassee and once belonged to a grand old plantation estate.

"Moon Island was a grand old estate a long time ago," said Pasquin. He sipped on the liqueur, emptying half the little glass at once. "It would be fine if somebody took hold of that old house and redid it, make it into a pretty white mansion where we could all sit on the porch and sip these things." He finished the glass and held it out for Rachel to fill it again.

"That would be just awful," she said. "I'd rather see the island sold and the money handed over to Sissy. That nasty old house should be torn down."

CHAPTER SEVENTEEN

I had insisted we leave before Iris and Pasquin had too much liqueur and wouldn't be able to make it home. Had I offered, Iris would have stayed at my place, but I couldn't take the woman's chatter right now. She took off in her car, waving and shouting that she'd be back for more recordings.

When I got home, there was a message from Vernon that he'd call if things looked quiet on the water. They must have been because he phoned an hour later.

"Corwin and his brother showed up at Mama's Table," I said.

"Yeah. They were in that little boat Sissy runs. I saw them headed back toward the island. From the stakeout there, that's where they ended up with about three bags from the restaurant."

"Take-out? At least Sissy will get her belly full tonight."

"You feel guilty about her, don't you?"

"Left to care for a senile old lady and not left with much to do it with, you bet."

"She's got a father who earns a living and doesn't abuse her," said Vernon. "That's about all the county cares about."

"Well, I tend to care a little more," I said.

"Don't get too close, Luanne." He sounded a bit monotone but lightened up when he said, "Plato can't use a sister."

He rang off when he heard another boat coming towards him on the river. I felt sorry for him having to deal with the boredom and the bugs. Sitting all night on the river with only a frog chorus for entertainment seemed an insult to someone who had so many years wearing the badge. I sighed, and like Vernon, chalked it up to being part of the job, and any job has its boredom quality. It was nearly dawn when my summation of his position was torn to shreds.

"He's where?"

Loman had called me on his cell phone from the emergency room. He was waiting to have some cuts on his own arms attended to while Vernon was in X-ray.

"He got belly whomped by some young kid, at least he was about the size of one. Just ran at him and busted his gut with his head. Vernon didn't see that coming."

"Where was he?"

"On the Craw Fish dock. The stakeouts saw a shrimp boat stop and lower a row boat. Couple of men got off, rowed to shore and met another man in a truck. Feds and deputies moved in, including Vernon who was trying to keep one guy from jumping back into the row boat."

"Who were they?"

"Illegals, we're pretty sure. Tony—Mr. Cuban descent—can't speak Spanish well enough and had to drag in Sergeant Jimenez."

"Tina Jimenez?" I smiled. Tony had his problems with me and with female deputies. Having to bring in Tina to interpret the language of his heritage must have bruised his ego.

"That's the one. Of course, we think maybe these guys speak some English, but they aren't admitting to it."

I promised to call the hospital to see if Vernon would be admitted. My reaction was to sit down and shiver. Vernon had never been subject to any problem like this before. Now he could be wounded, or at least too sore to dive. I closed my eyes and thanked the stars that he hadn't broken anything like Harry MacAllister had done with his leg inside a cave entrance. The experience with an underwater bomb had freaked Harry to the point that he basically gave up diving. Vernon was my hero both in and out of water.

"Brace up, Luanne," I told myself and headed for the coffee pot.

They let me see him that evening. Vernon's bald head had a bandage from getting a cut on some hauling equipment when the Hispanic man hit his middle like a cannon ball.

"Man wasn't quite five foot three," he said and tried to laugh. It came out as a moan. "I can't believe he knocked so much air out of me." He stopped talking to breathe and began again. "I've been hit in the belly before, but that just made me mad and I came back fists flying. This time, I hit my head and saw stars." He faced me and smiled.

"How did you get on that dock in the first place?" I said, trying to prevent my own eyes from watering. I needed distraction to avoid a total emotional outburst.

"We finally caught them. While everyone's attention was on the dock and unloading shrimp, a row boat came to take three men off the shrimper. Stakeout about a mile from me reported it. The two on closest stakeout managed to get on board and hold the pilot at bay. Another deputy from farther upriver got there in time to run after the man in the row boat. He was radioing for help when I saw him take off running through the woods. Tony said the man got away, but they got the dogs out there now.

"I climbed on the dock. The deputy who had the pilot at gunpoint, told me to come aboard and check below, but I had barely climbed on board when this ball of humanity flew at me. He may have been hiding on deck. "

"They're illegals, then?"

"Seems so. Three of them. The two on deck and a woman below."

"And the pilot?"

"Your friend," he said. "Sissy's father."

I sat down and held Vernon's hand. What else could happen to this child?

"I suppose he was trying to make you believe he was delivering shrimp to the dock?"

"He was," said Vernon. "He took advantage of that to make some extra money."

"Has he been arrested?"

"Of course. Transporting illegal aliens. He's in trouble with us and with the Feds."

I squeezed my eyes shut. Sissy can't stay out there with that senile woman. Not unless Aaron is around.

"What about the brother? You said he wasn't really in jail in Jacksonville."

"We don't know about him yet. He's suspect in these cases with illegals, too."

"Vernon, I have to go out there and see what's happening with Sissy. She'll be frantic if Mrs. Moon wanders off again, and heaven forbid something should happen to the old lady."

Vernon gave my hand a squeeze and frowned. "You could leave it to Children's Services."

I stared at the floor. The image of Sissy screaming as her "grandmother" is hauled off to a nursing home or worse, then she's dragged to foster care, gave me chills. She'd run away in no time and lose herself in the swamps.

"No, I feel somewhat responsible to check on her welfare," I said.

"Her welfare, for now," said Vernon. "Not forever."

Our goodbye-for-now may have been a bit excessive but no one saw us but a nurse who popped her head inside the room to let Vernon know he'd be getting a roommate within the hour.

"I need to be out of here," he said.

"I'll see what I can do," I said and went off to talk to a doctor.

There was no doctor available but I left my address and phone with the nurse at the station and told her Vernon would be going there when he was discharged. On the way home, I phoned Pasquin and told him to rev up the boat.

"So Mr. Corwin Moon got himself caught up in transporting illegals," said Pasquin after I had given him the story of the stake-outs and arrest. "We heard something went down on the river last night. Never knew it was your beau that got hurt."

"He'll be all right," I said. "I'm just thankful that guy had only a hard head and no gun."

"Or a knife," he said. "I once saw a man near 'bout gut a grown man. Stabbed him 'til he was unconscious and then cut him open. Some men grabbed his arms and stopped him, but he fought them like a bobcat."

"Where did you see that?" It sounded too much like a swamp story, the kind made up after too many swigs off the common bourbon bottle.

"Down near the river entry. Used to be an old bar down there, and these sailors got into some wild tussles with each other." He grinned. "That old fellow lived. Doctors sewed him up good. He said it cured his indigestion."

"Pretty much cured his digestion, too, I'll bet."

We pulled up to the dock at Moon Island. Even down near the

water, I could hear laughter coming from the porch. It was female laughter, one loud and lusty, the other high pitched and frantic.

"Looks like your professor got here on her own this time," said Pasquin. "Early bird, ain't she?"

We stood in the grassy clearing that served for a yard in front of the crumbling house. Iris and Beatrice sat in the rickety chairs and hooted about something. Iris' old recorder sat on an upturned crate near her big leather purse.

"The woman never gets enough," I said. "Must be nice to be so dedicated to one's profession."

"Oh, do come and listen to these stories," Iris said. She looked at Beatrice and asked the unanswerable. "Are there more chairs inside that we can bring out?"

Beatrice's eyes glazed over. She stared at Iris, then at me. When she saw Pasquin, her face beamed for a minute. She finally sat back and "spaced out," not knowing who anyone was at the moment.

"Oh, dear," said Iris. "She's doing a lot of that lately. I should know better than to keep asking her questions that she has to think about, like the extra chairs."

"She doesn't know about her own chairs?" said Pasquin.

"Mostly no," said Iris. "She hasn't taken care of a house for years. What's here or not here comes and goes in her head."

"I see you're still taping." I pointed to the recorder, its red light indicating everything we said was there.

"Sorry," Iris said and clicked it off. "We were having a conversation about some funny things that happened a long time ago. Telling jokes about her family leant itself to using that strange past tense." She patted the recorder. "I've got a bundle of it."

"Iris, Corwin has been arrested." I said it in front of Beatrice to see how she would react. She didn't.

Iris placed her hand over her mouth. She walked to the end of the porch and peered around it. "Sissy is back there with Trukee. They're shucking more oysters," she whispered. "Does she know?"

"She should but maybe not." I left the porch and walked to the back door that led to the kitchen.

Trukee had pulled a work table from somewhere and had set up two places to shuck oysters. With a bucket between them, Sissy worked one end of the table, Trukee the other.

"Where are these oysters coming from all of a sudden?"

"He's got a business now," said Sissy and nodded to her companion.

"Got me a little oyster boat and tongs," said Trukee. "Been wanting that for a long time. Just saved up the money to buy me an outfit."

"And you're doing your own harvesting now?"

He nodded and grinned and offered me a raw oyster on the half shell. I shook my head. From what I'd heard about this man, he worked the shrimp boats and spent what he made on something to send him to Never Never Land. Maybe I'd heard wrong about him, too. If Aaron hadn't been in jail, maybe Trukee hadn't been high most of his life.

"Sissy, I need to talk to you."

She looked up at me and frowned. "I heard already. They arrested Corwin."

"They arrested your father," I said.

"Yeah, Corwin," she nodded.

"Do you know the reason?"

"Don't you?" she gouged out the oyster with the little knife and plopped it in the bucket. They had a pile of shells building beneath the table.

"Yes, he was transporting people on a shrimp boat. People

who aren't supposed to be here."

"Illegals," she said. "He's been doing that for a while."

"I didn't hear that," I whispered to myself. I looked at Trukee who had stopped shucking for a moment to stare at me.

"Do you know this?" I said to him.

He shook his head and went back to the mollusk.

"I need some water," said Sissy. "You want some?" She asked Trukee who shook his head again. I followed her inside the kitchen.

"These old knives need replacing," she said and opened a drawer full of the oyster shucking instruments. Their wooden handles had faded, even changed shape, with years of use. The flat blades still had sharp pointed tips.

"Your family did a lot of this in the past, I gather?"

"Lots," said Sissy. "Grandma said they once had a shucking shed down near the boat dock."

"Sissy, we have to decide how to handle things." I bent over to look her in the face.

"No. I know I have to stay and take care of Grandma and Trukee and maybe rent out a room. Uncle Aaron plans on coming back tonight. He's always in charge if Corwin can't be around. That's been written in a paper."

"I see. You've never had a visit from Children's Services or been told you'll go to foster care."

"Never! And if they try, I'll run away. I don't live in heaven, but if I'm takened away, I'll die. And Grandma will die in a nursing home."

"Okay, okay. But, look, if you ever need a place to stay, I've got extra rooms."

She shook her head. "I won't do that to you. Nobody can stand Grandma like I can. When her mind goes blank, even Uncle Aaron stomps off. She stays here!" She slammed shut the oyster knife drawer and stamped one foot on the floor.

"You'd be a handful in a foster home," I laughed.

"More like a bucket full of lizards," she said and returned to the outside with a different knife and a glass of water.

I joined Iris and Pasquin on the front porch again.

"Miss Ant Bed is shucking oysters with her boarder," I said. "Seems he has bought himself a boat and tongs."

"How'd you get here, anyway," said Pasquin to Iris.

"I went to Fogarty Spring in hopes of talking to Rachel again, but I ran into Sissy coming out of the house. She offered to bring me in her boat."

"You want to ride back with us?"

"Well, I suppose I've got enough on tape for today." She leaned over to within a few inches of Beatrice's face. "Mrs. Moon, I'm leaving now. You should be okay sitting here for a while." She used two fingers to tilt the lady's chin toward her. Mrs. Moon's eyes moved and for a brief moment focused on Iris' face. "Sissy is out back. She's shucking oysters for your dinner."

Beatrice shook her head slightly and opened her eyes wide. "Is she using a knife?"

"I suppose she's using an oyster knife. Isn't that what she's supposed to do?"

Beatrice nodded slowly. "Yes. She's supposed to use an oyster knife." The sense left the eyes and she slumped again, gazing far off into the ether of her mind.

CHAPTER EIGHTEEN

"I'm glad we met up," said Iris as I drove her from my landing to Fogarty Spring. Pasquin had doffed his hat and taken off for a meeting with some of his cronies. "I've burnt the CD. Actually, two of them. You won't believe what I ended up doing to get it done. I had no idea how to get the information from my old cassette recorder to the computer. Took it by the computer lab on campus and a nice young man with terribly dirty fingernails did it for me. I thought you'd like to hear Rachel's accent. She's remarkably like her aunt, when she's talking and imbibing. Sober, she's too careful, and it shows. Over compensates sometimes with the accent."

"You mean she tries to over-Southernize it?"

"Sometimes, and she will do it until it sounds almost British. Quite comical, really. It was almost like she goes back in time from local to Southern USA to British pronunciations. I, of course, did not laugh, but I'll bet others have over the years."

"And she told you a lot about her life at Moon Island?"

"Not much, really. She just spoke about the legend of her relative and his encounter with the lake. She's heard a few stories. They're all about the same with some variation."

"Variation?"

"From being drunk and falling in, to going swimming and drowning, to running off to California with the daughter of a sailor." Iris laughed. "I'll bet that old guy was never as interesting as he's come to be on tape."

"Are you going to tape anyone else? I mean your sources are a captive audience, so to speak." I laughed at my own joke.

"Do you think they'd let me inside the jail with my recorder to listen to Corwin?" Iris sounded excited, another adventure into unknown lands.

"No. They won't unless…"

"Unless?"

"Unless they think something will be on the tape they can use. You'd need his lawyer's consent, too. Not likely to get it."

I pulled behind her car on the tiny main street of Fogarty Spring. She told me to wait while she ran to the trunk of her car.

"Here," she said and passed the two CDs to me. "Please let me know what you hear."

I said I would. She saluted and laughed.

On the way home, I began to wish I'd traded in the old Honda wagon for a new car like Tony suggested a few years back. It didn't have a CD player.

The evening could have been a drag had it not been for Beatrice's voice running from a monotone hoarseness to squealing delight to dramatic anger. Iris had given her free reign, had shut up and let her talk. The pattern of the odd past tense for "took" came up often, enough to want to explore whether or not it was used by other people living in the area. Not much else was there in peculiar dialect. A lot was there in what amounted to legend.

Beatrice began in a retelling of how she saw her husband, dear Oscar, walk into the water and never come up again. She sounded

quite sane when she said she didn't watch for him to come out of
the water, that she figured he'd surface and climb out and come to
the house in wet clothes. I wanted to ask why she'd say that, but
Iris, of course, didn't. The CD recording belonged to the way
Beatrice talked, not the information in her talk.

Once in a while, when Beatrice slowed down, Iris would say
"tell me again how it happened or tell me what other people say
about it," and she would start all over. Sometimes she'd tell the
same story in a disinterested monotone way. Other times she'd
get angry with her husband. *You had no right! You could swim. Why
didn't you come home?* It wasn't unusual until you realized it occurred
nearly fifty years ago. A spouse often gets angry when a mate dies.
Most get over it.

I stopped the player and stood at the sink to eat a supper of a
hamburger bun, coleslaw, and a warmed-over grouper filet. Washing it down with a soda, I sat on the porch and soaked in the
approaching night sounds. Two police boats went flashing by, their
new motors pushing against the current. A shrimp boat with a
delivery came chugging after them, followed by more police boats.
The Feds weren't taking any chances. I wondered what it would
be like, dirt poor with little food for the children or for an old lady
much like Beatrice, living in a rotten board house. Would I get on
a boat and head for the States? Of course, I would. I didn't like
the idea of starving. Hiding below on one of the shrimp boats,
doing everything to avoid the Feds—Federales—I'd be scared but
at least hopeful that things could change for a moment. At least
I'd be doing something.

Clouds came across the water and blocked out any light there.
When a streak of lightning flashed in the distance, I saw Plato
come running from the direction of Pasquin's house. He jumped
inside when thunder cracked the silence. I checked his wounded

leg and found no sign of infection.

With rain pouring down outside, I listened to more of the CD. Beatrice didn't complain about repeating the story. She used about the same amount of dialect as before, but her voice progressed from hoarse monotoned control to nearly hysterical. At one point, she introduced other elements into the story almost as though making up stuff, like a child who wanted to embellish a lie.

I watched from the window. Up there. The tree branch reached to the water. He was under it, I know. I just know. How? I just know. I could see feet off and on. Big feet. Bare feet. And arms. Brown arms. White arms. Brown and white. White arms without a body. Oscar in the water. He didn't try. Didn't even try to swim. He just sunk. Like a big rock. He sunk in that water. He's down there, you know. Pause. Most people come up again, but he takened himself down there and never came home again.

That story stopped. There must have been a rest. Iris' voice said, "Tell me again about the tree and Oscar's fall into the lake."

Beatrice started again, calm and repeating the first story. She said nothing more about the brown and white arms. I played that story again. Was it the ramblings of a demented woman, a mix-up of other events with the legend, or did something like that really occur? I stared at the CD. I wanted to ask Iris to question the woman about things, but I dared not. It wouldn't be the sample she wanted, and she might be offended that I wanted to use the recording for something other than her linguistic research.

I dozed on the couch, the rain coming down in a steady drumming on the roof. Plato didn't care. He dreamed on his blanket in a safe warm place. Was Sissy's home safe and warm?

The next day, I headed for my office after my first class. Iris was in the area.

"Looking at some of the data on dialects of that region," she said. "Not too much really." That pleased her. It wouldn't be easy to find something different after all these years of students doing field work.

I leaned against the wall next to the small library of graduate work. "Iris, I listened to Beatrice's CD. What do you think she meant by brown and white arms?"

She stopped and thought for a moment. "I don't know. Well, I did sort of make a guess. But, you know I'm not interested in the actual legend. Just the dialect."

"What did you sort of guess? Humor me."

"It was, after all, 1959. After slave days, true, but before the Civil Rights Law, and you know what the South was like. I figured there was a black man on the grounds somewhere, and she got him mixed up with her husband."

"I don't want to sound crude, but I never heard a biased Southerner refer to African American arms as brown. They would have said black—if not something worse."

"True," she said, and moved her head to the side in thought. "You know, I don't really know what she meant. Ah! Unless it was some sailor with dark tanned arms. Now I've seen those." She smiled, pleased that she solved a part that she didn't care much about anyway.

I shrugged. "She saw her husband go into the water and brown and white arms. Strange story."

"Oh, yes, strange," said Iris. "And I'm afraid a little wacky. That's why it's good to get the recordings now. I've known people with declining minds to totally shut up after a while."

There wasn't much use in trying to pry more from her. Hoping she would have enough curiosity to ask the next time she recorded the woman, I left to make a quick trip to the hospital.

Vernon was sitting up, his middle bound and his head looking nasty from the stitches. I examined it up close and shivered as I thought about his head striking something metal and sharp.

"They're discharging me this afternoon if all the tests look right," he said. "I'm supposed to be sore for quite a while, but I'm good to go."

"You're going with me, you know."

"I figured that. Just don't wear me out. I mean I'm not athletic right now."

"I won't make you play football," I smiled. "In fact, with those bandages, I'm likely to land you in the guest bed."

"Goody! Tell me again why I'm going home with you."

I told him the stories I heard on the CD, and about the brown and white arms.

"She's getting something mixed up, I'll bet," said Vernon. "You know it's not proven that he really went into the water. No one else saw him. Maybe he ran off with a 'brown' girl and Beatrice has told the lie so many times that she believes herself."

"I've got one more class today. I think I'll take some food out to Moon Island. They've got enough oysters for weeks, but they need some fresh fruit."

"You think you're fooling me, don't you?" Vernon smiled. "Get Pasquin to take you. I don't like the idea that Aaron hasn't been located yet." He looked at me and stopped smiling. "Take the gun, too, Luanne."

I promised to pick him up later, but he said he'd get Tony to do it and he'd take him to my house. "I need to be brought up on the case anyway."

Pasquin chuckled when I phoned him from the car.

"I'm going to start charging taxi service, woman!"

"Just meet me at the landing. I'll buy your dinner, even cook you one some day." I frowned at my own joke and thought about Sissy. I hated cooking on a routine basis. How could I even think of adding a preteen to my household?

I broke the speed limit on the highway and down the two-lane road to my house, slowing only when I saw the dead deer beside the road. Someone had hit it, but it could have been a trooper that pushed it to the side. The driver could have injuries to both himself and the car. I made a quick stop at a local farmer's stand and bought some produce: cantaloupe, grapes, tomatoes, and beans. I pulled into the carport. Pasquin rocked on the porch, his friend Edwin at his side.

"Thought we'd both go," Pasquin said. "Edwin and I will keep the boat company while you visit with the kid."

Edwin, the swamp man with a preference for snakes over people, grinned and nodded. He didn't say much and gave the impression of the local idiot, but those of us who lived here knew better. He held up a six pack of beer and a long salami stick.

"Now tell me, Edwin. What do you know about the snakes around Moon Island?" I asked.

"Whoo-boy! Don't get him started," said Pasquin. "That's why he wants to go. Says there's some kind of oak snake on that island that has a different coloring from those around here."

Another oddity, I thought. Not even the snakes are normal. I ran upstairs and changed clothes. We climbed into Pasquin's boat, avoiding the snake pole and bucket that Edwin used to capture his hobbies live. "I'm not riding back in this boat with a live snake," I said. They both laughed.

Pasquin edged his way around a grassy area where baby alligators half floated on the water surface. If it appeared that he was disturbing their resting place, Mama Gator would be after us, her watchful eyes following us far out into the river. The image of Sissy alone on that river didn't escape me. Who was her Mama Gator?

Sissy sat on the dock, her feet hanging over the side. Her face and hair were dirty, and she looked tired.

"Grandma is sleeping finally. She's been difficult today. I think she understands about Corwin being arrested."

"It can't be easy for a grandmother to hear something like that. Is Trukee here?"

"Not yet. He went off to the oyster beds. I'll be shucking those things again tonight."

I introduced her to Edwin who tipped an imaginary hat. She stared at the man when I told her about his expertise. She finally smiled and said, "You can take all the snakes you want off this island. Dead or alive. I don't care."

Edwin didn't get the joke and thanked her. "It'll be live ones if I take any," he said. He grabbed his bucket and pole and strode away from the direction of the house.

Pasquin leaned back in the boat. He opened a beer and sipped slowly. "Don't let the river patrol know I'm doing this."

Sissy and I carried the produce bags to the house. She seemed relaxed that someone had actually arrived to talk to her. Aaron still had not made an appearance.

"Luanne," said Sissy when we put the bags on the porch, "do you think Uncle Aaron could be dead?"

Inside I shivered. The thought had crossed my mind. "No evidence of it so far. Why do you ask?"

"He worked on the shrimp boats. Did deliveries just like Corwin did." She placed her hands on her hips and pouted. "Wouldn't surprise me if he wasn't doing the same stuff."

"Like transporting illegal aliens?"

She nodded. "Why is it so bad?"

"Just because it's against the law," I said. "The poor guys are looking for work, but they don't have permission to be here."

She gave out a loud sigh. "Well, why don't they give them some permissions and let them work?"

"It's out of our hands, Sissy." I backed away from the porch and looked up to the roof. "Do you have any idea how old this place really is?"

She joined me in the yard. "Not really. Somebody said it got started during the Civil War. Corwin says it was before that even."

"How many rooms in all?"

She shrugged. "I don't know 'cause it's dangerous to climb over on that side. The boards are rotten."

"Termites, I suspect. And the attic? There must be one with a pointed roof like that."

"Yeah, and it's full of dusty stuff. I used to go up there when the ladder still worked."

"The ladder?"

"One of those that pulls down. It has steps on it and you can climb up there. I haven't done it in a few years. Corwin says it's not safe."

I looked at her and grinned as childish as I knew how. "Want to try it again? While no one is looking?"

"You won't tell?" She grinned back at me.

"Not on your life."

We climbed to a hallway not far from Beatrice's room. Even with the door closed, her loud snoring bounced off the old boards.

"There." Sissy pointed to a broken piece of rope hanging from a rusted hook in the ceiling. She brought a footstool and waited for me to climb on it.

"How did you reach the rope?" I asked as I stood on tiptoe and barely touched the rotten end.

"I got the big ladder we used to keep up here. And the rope was longer then."

With a yank, I pulled on the rope. The rotted strings broke but not before pulling the steps down enough for me to get my fingers in and pull it all the way down. Dust floated into the hallway.

I started to climb when Sissy said to wait. She ran into the bathroom and came out with two hand towels.

Upstairs would have thrilled an antique dealer and horrified a fireman. If ever Sissy inherited the place, she could finance her college education on some of the furniture here.

"I think this was Grandpa Oscar's desk," she said, her voice muffled by the cloth.

"It's a beaut," I said and pulled on the drawers. Someone had broken the locks on all of them.

"Grandma came up here once and went kind of crazy with a crowbar. That was the last time Corwin let me roam around here. Said she might hit me with it."

"Was she angry?"

"Yeah. She'd pry open the drawers and hit them, ripped up all the papers. I think she burned them out back."

I stared at the desk over my face cloth. Dust was everywhere, and some of it was mixed with mildew. I pulled open one empty drawer.

"I think I heard her get up," said Sissy and tiptoed toward the stairs.

All the drawers were empty. Beatrice's anger had made a complete job of removing her husband's papers, photos, bills, what else? Below, we heard Beatrice move from her room to the bathroom.

"Come on!" said Sissy. "She'll tell or want to come up here herself."

I followed her down the stairs and shoved it upward from the stool. It slammed, but maybe Mrs. Moon hadn't heard it.

She had heard something, but our stars blessed us. She thought it was someone coming in the front door.

"Nothing but wind, Grandma," said Sissy. "Corwin needs to fix the screen again." Necessity had taught her how to lie.

CHAPTER NINETEEN

"He bit you?" I stood on the dock in disbelief. Edwin sat with a handkerchief—and I wouldn't swear to its sanitary state—wrapped around his hand.

"He's not poisonous," Edwin said and lifted one half of the snake bucket lid. Something enormous twisted in the bottom.

"Good God! That thing is big as a boa."

"It's an oak snake," said Pasquin. "Ill tempered things that grow several feet long." He began to laugh between his words. "You should have seen Edwin's face when he came running with a heavy bucket in one hand, the other waving at me like I was going to leave him. Won't be the first time some old reptile got his teeth in Edwin's limbs."

"Is there any way the thing can get out of that bucket?" I sat at the other end of the boat, next to Pasquin and the tiller.

"Not unless I open up both sides of the lid and show him the way." Edwin patted the bucket that rested—if one could say what was inside provided any rest—next to his leg.

"Like it or not, Edwin, we're stopping at the Fogarty Spring clinic before anybody goes home." I looked at Pasquin. "I mean it. We may not be dealing with poison but heaven knows what kind of bacterial infection he could get."

"Snake will sooner die than Edwin will." But Pasquin didn't argue.

Pasquin's slow pace felt like eternity, and when we caught up with the Jesus Saves boat, it really was eternity. The preacher's voice scattered birds and turtles as it echoed across the surface of the river, telling bugs and fish how sinful they were and they must repent to find everlasting life. At one point, it swerved too fast and the man's voice, caught clearly by his microphone, shouted "Whoa!" His hand pressed over the speaker couldn't mask some mumbling in the background that sounded a whole lot like cursing at the pilot.

Pasquin began to laugh. It was catching. All three of us nearly howled when we slowly passed the dressed up boat.

"Think we should show him what we found in the Garden of Eden?" said Pasquin as he pointed to Edwin's bucket.

"Don't you dare open that thing!" I said and instinctively brought my legs up and sat lotus style.

Edwin giggled and, thankfully, didn't open the lid. Instead, Pasquin raised his empty beer can in a salute to the preacher and said, "a la sante, Preacher Man" as we passed his end of the boat. He stared at us and kept off the microphone until we were out of sight around a bend. We heard him continue speaking, finding the ears of dumb critters much better members for his congregation.

We passed my landing and docked in Fogarty Spring. The clinic, which catered mostly to river injuries, was within walking distance.

"How many times have you been here with snake bites, Edwin?" The young doctor who volunteered three evenings a week ordered a shot and some bandaging.

"Never counted them," he said. "This one kind of hurt 'cause the snake was big. Them oaks got an evil temper."

"Maybe they don't like being dragged away from their favorite tree and stuck in a bucket, not to mention taken away from a great source of food."

I paced the floor. Pasquin waited in the tiny lobby. He didn't like watching people get shots. "Edwin, do you know how many rats the Moon house might get because you took away this reptile?"

"Oaks prefer birds to rats."

"You asked one, I suppose?"

He winced when the nurse dabbed on some medicine, then grinned at me. "They never do answer me."

It was a clever retort in spite of his brain capacity. Someone must have told him that joke and he kept it in his mental folder.

I tossed up my hands and joined Pasquin. "Look. You take him and that snake home. I'll stick around Mama's Table. You come right back and take me home. I need to meet Vernon at the house. He's getting out of the hospital tonight."

Pasquin stood and bowed. "Is he ready?"

The doctor handed Edwin a bottle of antibiotics to take as a precaution. He wouldn't take them. Once in his dining room I had seen dozens of prescribed pill bottles, still full.

I watched as the two men drifted off to Pasquin's boat. Taking a longer path from the clinic to Mama's Table at the dock, I passed Rachel's house deliberately. With any luck, she'd be on her porch or making her dinner.

"My goodness, I never expected you," she said when I rapped on the screen door.

"It's a long story, but I never meant to be here, either." I sat in her close living room and told her the story of Edwin and the oak snake.

"Such daring!" she gasped, doing her Southern belle act that made Iris want to laugh. "A bit foolish, but daring."

"A bit stupid if you ask me."

I drank some water. "I won't stay long. Pasquin will be back in a few minutes to take me home. You know, I'm a linguistics professor, too, and Iris has let me listen to Beatrice's tapes."

"Will you listen to mine, also?"

"Oh yes. She needs another ear to make sure she's got the patterns right."

"I'm not quite sure what that means, but it is most interesting." The act was getting worse. I figured Miss Rachel had sipped a few in the preparation of her seafood stew.

"Mrs. Moon mentioned something in one of her tales about her husband, something about brown and white arms. Does that ring a bell with you?"

Rachel frowned and stayed silent for a few moments. "Not a single chime," she said. "I'm sure she's mixing up legends. There are others, you know. That old house has passed down more tall tales than any fiction writer."

"Were there ever any people with brown arms around the place?"

She shook her head and shrugged. "Far as I know, most of the sea going fellows had tans, some pretty deep, but no one else until now."

"You mean Patel?"

"Is that his name? He's that East Indian fellow that was living there for a while. Sissy said he moved on."

"Yes, he did." I didn't tell her how far he'd moved on. "But I'm talking about long ago, when Oscar went into the lake."

She pressed a hand to her lips and shook her head.

"You never had black people working around the place?"

"There were some, but they had black arms, not brown."

I left and trotted to the landing. Pasquin had just pulled up to the stairs that led off the dock.

"Who has brown arms, Pasquin? I mean who had brown arms back in the days when old Man Moon dropped off the side of the lake?"

He fanned himself with his hat and guided the boat into the river lane. "Only person I know is Gavi. He's got that Portuguese blood and naturally brown coloring."

I didn't continue that line. Gavi was there, watching the radiant teenage Rachel preen in front of the boats before diving off into the water. Did he make it off the boat and take out the old man with his brown arms? Or maybe he took the lovely Rachel and Beatrice saw him do it? I shook my head in the breeze as we headed to my landing.

Pasquin sat down in the boat and told me to wait a minute when I tried to climb out. "Did Gavi do something I need to know about?"

"Not that I know of. It's just that I'm trying to penetrate Mrs. Moon's mind. She wasn't talking about Gavi, I'm almost sure."

I pulled myself on the dock. As Pasquin pushed away, he calmly said, "Don't be telling me fibs, ma'am."

Before I could settle onto my couch, the phone rang.

"I'm getting out but can't be there until later. If it's not too late, I may need you to come and get me."

"From where?"

"Sheriff's department. We got a meeting going with the Feds. May be some action tonight."

"Vernon! You're in no condition for action."

"I know. I'll be right here, manning the action from a desk."

I rested, trying not to wonder how a department could put a man right out of the hospital back on duty, even if it was on the desk. I pressed the Play button and tried to involve myself with

Beatrice's voice again, listening to that tale over and over, trying to pick out the tiny changes each time. In the first version, Oscar was disgusted with something on the front porch. He threw it down and went to the lake and jumped in—not likely. Eventually, he argued with one of his sons, cursed and walked into the lake— could be he did argue with someone. Finally, he was resting under the tree, cooling off from a hot day, and gave up and jumped into the water. And never came up? Did he perhaps swim to the other side, underwater, and crawl out where no one saw him? Did he have someone waiting in a boat that would take them both out to open ocean and off to California?

I wanted someone to sit down with Mrs. Moon and ask her to talk about Mr. Moon, not the legend of his disappearance but what he was like prior to that time. Beatrice's hysterical voice lulled me into a troubled sleep. I awoke when Plato barked from outside. Someone was pounding on the door.

"Me and this here hound walked all the way over," said Pasquin. "Couldn't take the boat. They blocked off the river 'tween there and here." He fanned himself and sat in a rocker.

"Come inside where it's cooler."

"Better out here. I don't like to cool down in cold air. Not good for the joints." Plato agreed with him and lay at his feet.

"From the looks of both of you, you ran through those woods."

"I wondered what you'd be up to, but I guess you don't even know what's going on." He took a deep breath and stopped panting. "I could have called but I wanted to see how far down the river this thing went."

"What thing?"

"They got all kinds of patrol boats with bright lights surrounding a shrimp boat out there. Got men on shore shining lights in the trees. Your dog was visiting and got all excited. He's as pooped as I am."

"Did they find anyone in the trees?"

Pasquin shrugged. "I locked up the house and walked here. I didn't see or hear anyone. Dog came with me and didn't notice anyone, either."

"I guess that's what Vernon meant when he said there would be some action tonight. They must have caught more illegals on one of the shrimp boats, and if Corwin is in custody, he's not the pilot of this one."

"Illegals?"

I had forgotten that Pasquin had not been privy to that part of the situation. He knew Patel was dead but he didn't know why.

"No wonder there's Fed boats out there, too."

"I'll bet there are a hundred swamp eyes peeping at the river about now. You'll have lots to talk about over the bourbon bottle tomorrow night."

With the river blocked off, the usual inhabitants couldn't get home and two of them tied up at my landing. They heard us talking and joined us on the porch. Without a single bark, Plato was wagging his tail and licking hands.

"He knows these guys?" I looked at Pasquin who moved chairs for two men who smelled a lot like fish that had been out of water a few hours too long.

"He comes to parties, too, sometimes," laughed one man who rubbed his knuckles over Plato's head.

"We've given him some rides down this way two or three times," said the other. "He'll take a boat ride any day before trotting off down that swamp path."

The four of us and Plato sat on the front porch. I didn't say much while the men speculated about what could have happened on the river. Pasquin kept his mouth shut about the illegals, but the men recognized the federal boats and knew it had to be big.

"Probably some giant drug bust from Central America," said one.

"Could be an agent got ambushed," said the other. "That happened once."

"When?" asked Pasquin.

"Back in the forties," he answered. Their throaty laughs echoed up and down the dark swamp.

I served iced tea and finally worked myself into the conversation by getting them to tell a little history of the river. I'd heard it all from Pasquin, many times, but nothing better suits an old fisherman than to tell stories of the past.

"And did any of you ever tie up at Moon Island?" I sipped on my tea to hide my face and to avoid Pasquin's eyes.

"Oh, yeah. That used to be a hoppin' place long before our time I hear tell. We tied up there a lot. Even took a cool dip in that lake."

"We used to call it the sailor's bathtub," laughed the other one. "Lots of men jumped in that place to wash off the days of sticky fish and salt air." He leaned his nose close to his lifted shoulder. "I could use a dip right now."

"Did you ever see the Moon family?" I asked when they finished laughing at their latest joke.

"Saw the boys a lot. They would swim with us. Used to see Mrs. Moon stand on the hill or on the porch. She'd keep an eye on us. I think she was afraid we'd sneak off up to the house and grab one of her girls."

"And did you?"

The two men stopped talking. Had it been daylight, I may have seen some blushing.

"Not there," one said. "Later on, they all got free of her and high-tailed it out of there. Not a one stayed faithful to their husbands." Laughter burst on the scene again.

"Where did they go?"

"Left with other fishermen, got jobs in town, who knows? I'll bet we don't know where a one of them is now."

"Except Miss Rachel Moon," said Pasquin. "She lives in Fogarty Spring."

"Yeah, Miss Rachel Moon," said the first man who began to stroke Plato's back as he talked. "Pretty red hair. She'd swim, too, but only when the men got out. Mrs. Moon wouldn't let any of them girls get near the place long as men were about." He chuckled. "She didn't know we were on board the boats and watching every move."

The other man leaned back in his chair and became part of the shadows. "Miss Rachel knew what we were doing. Paraded that pretty body and hair around like a bathing beauty on the beach. You know, she had the prettiest yellow suit, tight, and kind of crinkled around the front." He started to gather up the tail of his dirty shirt.

"She's not wearing that suit much lately," Pasquin chuckled.

"Guess not. She's as old as we are. Wonder if she still swims. She used to come out from under that big old oak, stand there and stretch, and dive just like a pretty white egret going after a fish."

"And oh boy when she got out!" They all laughed again. I had become background, the woman who didn't hear.

"I guess none of you had cameras." I interrupted the male bonding, and they stopped for a few seconds, kind of like a moment of silence before changing the tone.

"Couldn't afford cameras back then. Can't much afford them

now." A peal of laughter broke out again. Even Plato tired of it and begged to be admitted to the air conditioned living room.

"Funny people, those Moons," said Pasquin. "Only the old lady, two grandsons and a great granddaughter are left. Rachel, too, if you count living in the area."

"How come she never married?" asked one of the men who had as much condensation on his face as on his tea glass.

Pasquin shrugged. "Nobody good enough for her, I guess. Lots of college girls don't marry." He looked my way and I gave him the evil eye.

"Pretty ones like that do. And Rachel sure was pretty. She never let that soft white skin get burned. Always got her a towel and a big hat when she walked up the hill after her swim. Wrapped that towel around her tight." He laughed to himself.

When a police boat pulled up to the landing, the talk stopped and we waited for Loman to stumble across the road and tell them they could go around the scene now. Pasquin went with them instead of walking all the way home through dark woods.

"Tony says you should come to the office tomorrow while they're interrogating Corwin Moon. He'll call when he needs you."

CHAPTER TWENTY

Calling me when he needed me meant a vibration on my cell phone right in the middle of class. I stepped into the hall.

"Can you make it here?" Tony asked. "We'd like you here to back us up when we give him the times we know he was on the river."

"I can't swear it was Corwin piloting the boats," I said.

"We don't expect you to. He doesn't know you can't identify him. We've told him we have a witness to his being on the river in that boat at that time of night. We just need you to sit there. He'll get the picture."

"Are you sure? Sounds pretty iffy to me."

Tony didn't care. He had a plan, and I wasn't going to argue a chance to hear what was happening.

"Where's Vernon?" I asked. "Loman said he was busy and wouldn't be coming to my place at all last night."

"We had a deputy take him home this morning. He's in his own bed for now." Tony sounded irritated. "Look, Luanne, I need Vernon in condition to dive and I'm not going to wear him out doing other stuff. He volunteered to work the desk on this case. He should have gone home when he was discharged."

At least we agreed on that. "I'll be there as soon as this class ends."

The interrogation hadn't begun yet. Tony wanted it to run as he planned, and my presence was necessary at the beginning. Corwin had been placed in the room, his court appointed lawyer beside him.

"I'm going to take you in there, ask the man a question, ask you a similar question, and escort you out. Got that?"

I nodded and didn't have a chance to find out what the question would be. He held my arm and pushed me in front of him as he opened the door. Telling me to stand at the end of the table, he pushed the record button and made the preliminary statement about the interrogation.

"Now, Mr. Moon, do you know this lady?" Tony grabbed my arm again. He couldn't tell the difference between a witness and a suspect at this point as his fingers dug into my flesh.

Corwin looked at me, his weary eyes ready to water any minute. He hadn't combed his thin hair in hours. He nodded.

"Who is she?"

"Luanne Fogarty. She's visited with my daughter a few times."

"Where does she live?"

Corwin looked puzzled and turned to his lawyer who nodded. "On the Palmetto River, above the Palmetto Springs Park but before Fogarty Spring."

"You'd be able to find her house from the river, right?"

He nodded. Tony glared at him, and he said "yes."

"Luanne, do you know this man?" I said yes and identified him by name. That was it. No questions on where he lived or anything else. He told me to wait in the other room.

I sat in the two-way mirror room. Loman took a seat next to Tony in the interrogation room after he introduced his Sergeant.

"Mr. Corwin, I'm not going to question you about the illegal

aliens found on your shrimp boat or on the boat you were piloting that night. That's up to the federal agents. I'm going to question you about the death of one Mr. Kumar Patel, a boarder at
your house. When your boat was searched, we found some blood
in a spot which is usually washed clean with water. Now it's going
to take some time to do the DNA, but let me ask you this: will it
be Mr. Patel's blood?"

"How the hell should I know?" Corwin's eyes narrowed in his
unshaven face. His face, reddened, showing white skin at the hair-
line where he would wear a cap to keep out the sun's rays.

"Don't you know who gets on the boat?"

Corwin started to stand, but his lawyer motioned him back
into his seat. "Look," he said, "the boat isn't mine. I pilot it for a
private shrimping company. Lots of people come on board; some
of them are foreign like Mr. Patel. If you're asking me if he's ever
been on that boat, I'd say it was possible. He hired out on shrimp
boats. That was his profession."

"If it is his blood, it would have had to be the day we stopped
you, right?"

He shrugged.

"You hose down the boat after a run, don't you?"

"Always."

"Since the blood was found there, it would have to have been
deposited there after the hose down, right?"

"I don't know. What you're asking isn't within my expertise
with shrimp boats. To my knowledge no one has had an accident
lately."

The lawyer leaned forward. "He's answered your question, sir.
I'm going to tell him to stop until DNA analysis is offered. I'm
also going to state that I don't believe there really is any blood."

Tony sighed, turned red, and ground his jaw. He stood and

paced, working his mind at how to proceed next.

"Have you ever seen Luanne Fogarty on her landing when you're taking a delivery up the river?"

"Yes."

"Did you at any time shine your spotlight on her dock to see if she was there?"

"If I shined it, it wasn't to see if she was there. I have to look out for small boats that might dart out from landings. I use the spotlight sometimes when it's too dark to see anything."

Corwin was clever. He must have suspected now why I had been called in and identified.

"And do you ever kill your engine in the middle of your trip?"

Corwin stared at Tony, gave a sneer, and said "That wouldn't be too smart, would it?"

"And you're a good pilot, aren't you?"

"Good enough to know I'm not killing my engine in the middle of a run. I've had a problem a couple of times when the engine killed itself."

"Recently?"

"No. Once on another river. Once in the middle of the ocean."

Corwin leaned back and attempted to stretch. His lawyer touched him lightly on his arm.

"How long are you keeping me here?"

"We've got some more questions."

The give and take went on like this for over two hours. Corwin would become irritable, his lawyer would calm him and threaten to stop everything, Tony would change the question. Finally, the lawyer put a stop to everything.

Rushing back to campus, I finished my last class and headed home, hoping to see Vernon on my porch. Sissy was there instead, not on the porch but on the bottom step. Her eyes had the weariness of an old woman. Next to her was a rolled up towel.

"I want to swim today if you've got time."

I sat next to her and finally put my arm around her. "You're tired, aren't you?"

"Yeah. Grandma couldn't sleep and kept walking around and talking to herself. She worries me when she does that. She might fall."

"Is there anyone with her now?"

"Trukee just came in from his oyster haul. He said he'd watch her while I took a break. She was asleep when I left."

"Will he? I mean doesn't he kind of indulge himself at times?" I wasn't sure if Sissy knew what that meant, but I needn't have worried.

"He smokes joints sometimes, but never when he's watching her."

"Okay," I said. "Let's go inside and get our suits on."

Sissy hadn't forgotten anything I'd taught her. In fact, she caught on to making her own swimming moves.

"Can you teach me to dive with the tank?" she asked, treading water that was well over her head. She seemed fearless.

"Eventually, I suppose. You can start using a mask now." I retrieved an old one from the carport and showed her how to wear it. She looked like a maturing tadpole as she scooted underwater seeing clear sights of bottom snails. She had the bravery and curiosity that took me back years with my father in this same part of the river.

"I guess I'd better get back," she said as she rested her arms on the top step of the landing ladder. "If Grandma wakes up and goes nuts trying to find me, Trukee won't know what to do."

"Sissy, how did he save enough money to buy that oyster boat?"

She shrugged. "It's probably an old thing. The cabin is made from plywood he said. Some oyster man needed the money and sold it cheap, I guess."

"I still have that oyster knife that belongs to you," I said.

"Forget it. We have a drawer full. Don't need another one."

We dressed, and I gave her a snack of peanut butter and crackers. Refreshed from a successful swim and some food, not to mention time away from elder care, she looked like a child again. I hated sending her off to Moon Island, but she had to go before dark as far as I was concerned.

"A lot was going on up the river last night," I said. "You could run into police boats."

"I know," she said. "I heard they raided a boat and arrested a whole bunch of illegals."

"How did you hear that?"

"Just heard it," she shrugged and stood to go home. It was the reaction I often got from people who lived in the swamp. They told each other things but never confessed the source. I guessed some other shrimper had stopped by and told Trukee, a guess as good as any other.

Before Sissy could load a bag of oranges that I had given her into her boat, my cell phone rang.

"We're headed for Moon Island," said Tony. "We've got some information that the other boarder knows something. You want to meet us there and maybe help out with the girl and the old lady?"

"Better yet," I said. "I'll come with her."

Sissy's boat couldn't be pushed too hard. We'd end up going nowhere and calling for help if the engine stalled. Her face grew old again and she bit her lip as she guided us toward the mouth of the river.

"What will happen to Corwin and Trukee?" she asked after a

long silence.

"I don't know. Depends on whether or not they actually did anything."

"They did," Sissy said under her breath. "I'm sure they did."

"You don't think they hurt anyone, do you?"

She shook her head and ended the conversation.

Tony, Loman, and two federal agents stood on the front porch. Trukee was in a chair, his face as white as one of his shucked oysters. Sissy took one look and darted inside. I heard her feet slap against the stairs.

"Where is Mrs. Moon?" I asked.

"She's still sleeping," said Trukee. "She had a bad night, and when that happens, she pretty much sleeps all day." He gave me a half smile as though he was happy to see someone who might be a friend.

Tony pulled me to the other end of the porch, thought better of it and said, "Let's go into the yard."

We walked halfway down the bank toward the lake. A little farther and we'd be in the line of sight for anyone in Beatrice's room.

"We arrested Aaron last night. He and his brother have been taking payment to ship illegals upriver to the people who meet them and take them to secret houses. Seems the Mexican pilots collect money from the aliens, put them on boats, then transfer them to some shrimp boats in open ocean. At night, they deliver the men along with the shrimp."

"Sissy will end up in foster care for sure." I walked away from him for a moment. "And Patel informed on them, but they found out and killed him. Is that the scenario?"

"That's what we're working on. We also found out that Trukee got the money for his oyster boat from Corwin. He didn't borrow it. Corwin gave it to him, or perhaps paid him for something."

"Has he said anything yet?" I nodded toward the front of the house.

"Not yet. We're letting the Feds talk to him about the illegals first. We need a good cause to search the house, and if he hints of anything like murder, the judge will jump at it."

"Tony," I sighed and kicked myself inside for being on both sides of this situation. "Patel was killed with an oyster knife, the one Plato found, right?"

"Punched right in the carotid. Must have been blood squirting everywhere."

"I've been inside this house many times, and a few times in the kitchen. There is an entire drawer full of oyster knives. All anyone would have to do is grab one and walk out the door."

"Trukee is pretty good with one of those knives, at least with oysters. He'd know what kind of wound it would make."

"Given the history of this family with seafood, I'd expect every last one of them to know what an oyster knife would do."

"Even the kid?"

"Not her, Tony," I closed my eyes. Patel wasn't a tall man but he was too tall for Sissy to reach his neck with a short bladed knife unless he was sitting down.

"We're looking for motive, Luanne. Her father has the best one. Or her uncle."

Trukee still sat in his chair, but he stretched his neck to watch as Tony and I came around the side of the porch. The agents stood, leaning against the support columns which looked to me as though the bottoms, rotted and loose, might let go at any moment. Loman leaned against the wall next to the screen door. Bits of chipped paint rubbed off and stuck to his dark coat.

"Mr. Trukee," said Tony, "do you know where Mr. Patel went

when he left here?"

Trukee shook his head and gripped the arms of his chair.

"Did you help Corwin and Aaron kill him."

"No!" He screamed. "You won't pin that on me. I don't kill people."

"Then who does?" Tony smiled. At least now he knew that Trukee was aware that Patel was dead.

"Someone pretty damn crazy, I'd think!"

CHAPTER TWENTY-ONE

Rachel Moon sighed heavily before she started to speak. Tony had convinced her to either stay with Beatrice and Sissy on Moon Island or to offer them beds in her own house. She refused to the point of screaming at him that she had no intention of sleeping in that dirty boarding house and getting bug bites all over her skin. In the end, she put Beatrice in the spare room and Sissy on the couch.

"You are the only relative around, Miss Moon," said Tony. "Don't you see it as a responsibility even if it's temporary?" It worked.

"Sissy will have to stay around," she said. "She can't go roaming off in that boat and leave me alone with this woman. We never cared much for each other. Besides, I need to make a trip to buy groceries."

I shrugged and looked at Tony. "She stays with the old lady most of the time. And being here in Fogarty Spring, she's got a telephone and people around if she needs help. Let Rachel do her stuff as long as she's here at night."

"We're going to question all three men tonight," said Tony. "Grab Vernon and bring him in if he wants to hear it." He couldn't bring himself to give me a direct invitation. I would have to accompany Vernon. I nodded.

I checked my watch. It was nearly nine and would be dark in a few minutes. Rachel would have to travel several miles to find a supermarket open this late. I suspected it was a ploy to be out of the house as long as possible. Beatrice settled quietly in the spare bedroom, her eyes staring far away. Sissy had brought an old duffle bag with their night things and some medicines for the old lady. Before I left, she called after me.

"Give this to Corwin. Please." She lifted an orange and placed it in my hand.

I nodded, knowing the deputies wouldn't let me give him anything. I'd try anyway. It was the first gesture of friendliness toward her father I'd ever seen.

Vernon and I arrived at the department around ten. Tony was still setting things up, and waiting for Corwin's lawyer.

"We'll question everyone separately," he said. "But I'm starting with Corwin." He turned to Vernon, "If you think of anything you want asked, send word."

Vernon smiled as Tony left the observation room. "He means you, too, you know."

Waiting Room would have been a more apt name for our observation post. Corwin's lawyer had issues with coming to the department this late, but Tony finally convinced him that the Feds were itching to get at him, and he couldn't hold off any longer. All of which wasn't exactly true. The Feds were hoping Tony would pull everything both agencies needed from the man.

At eleven, everyone finally settled into their chairs. Tony did his preliminaries with the recording device. Corwin looked as though he hadn't slept in weeks. His hands shook. I patted the orange in my shirt pocket, determined to find a way for him to have it.

"We've got two of your buddies in custody, Mr. Moon. Well, one buddy named Trukee and the other your brother."

Corwin sat up as though he wanted to be defiant, but his face said otherwise. He was weary. His lawyer was disgusted.

"Ask!" he said to Tony. "And you don't have to say anything," he said to his client.

Corwin nodded.

"Do you want to tell us what you did with Mr. Patel's body?"

"Nothing!"

This line went on for an hour. I knew it wouldn't end for a long time, but I wasn't going to miss it. I left the room to call Manny, the linguistic department chair about the next day.

"Can you just go into the room, put this topic on the board and tell them to write the essay and leave it at my office?" I sounded like a nagging mother. Manny never liked to do the "teacher work" as he called it. He preferred that we call each other for this type of assignment, but he was the only one I could count on being awake.

"You owe me, Luanne." That was his agreement, and I hoped it meant he would actually see that it got done. I read the topic to him. I could hear the computer keys and hoped he wouldn't forget to print it out and take it in the next day.

"Some people should know when to retire," I said as I walked back into the observation room. "Anything new?"

"Corwin's not feeling too good. He's sweating and fidgeting. Tony needs to get on with it or the lawyer is going to call a halt."

"You paid Trukee, didn't you? Paid him enough to buy an oyster boat if he'd help you dump the body in a deserted area of the river. Didn't you?"

Corwin's face grew red. He beat both fists on the table and put his head down. In a hoarse voice that sounded almost like his grandmother's, he yelled, "All right! I dumped the body, but I didn't kill him. I'd never do that! I dumped him because I found him on my property and I didn't want trouble."

The lawyer stood up but Corwin pushed him back into his chair. "You got the illegals. Ask them. It had to be one of them who killed him. He was just there, next to the lake. We figured it would lead to discovering the other job. We had to get rid of him."

"The other job? You mean transporting illegals?"

Corwin nodded.

Tony excused himself and left the room. We watched as the lawyer attempted to whisper to his client, but Corwin shoved him away again. He rubbed his eyes and crossed his fingers behind his neck.

Tony came into our room. "He's lying. We checked on the aliens we caught. They were most likely not anywhere near the coast of Florida when Patel was killed."

"There are others here. What about the two women who disappeared when Sanchez died? If the word travels fast enough, one of them could have fingered him as a plant." Vernon argued with Tony for the sake of covering all angles.

"He says he found the body on his land. He and his brother and this Trukee haul it on board and dump it upriver. He hasn't said a word about knowing the guy was a plant, and he may not know."

"He was scared that you'd find out about the illegals if you knew about the body," I said. "Remember, he was totally nude when we found him." I looked at Tony who stared back and walked out of the room. We watched as he sat again in front of Corwin.

"What did you do with the man's clothes?" he asked.

Corwin didn't hesitate. "Trukee burned them. He helped put the body on the boat, but he didn't go with me. He took all the man's clothes, even the ones in his closet, to a barrel fire some-where on the bay and tossed them in, so he said."

Tony nodded as though he already knew this.

"And Aaron? What was his role?"

"He was already heading to another job in the Gulf. I called him on a cell phone. He agreed that I should dump the body somewhere, just get it off our island."

"And you paid Trukee?"

He nodded. "Enough to pay for that piece of junk boat. That's all he wants in life. Harvest a few oysters and smoke pot."

Tony leaned back in his chair and stared at the man. Corwin's big hands were shaking. They were red and nearly raw from the work he did. He wore a short sleeved prison shirt that fit tight over red, hairy arms. He didn't tan in the sun, but reddened up to the sleeve line. I imagined he would be pale white above that.

"Arms!" I whispered loud enough for Vernon to hear. "Get Tony back in here."

Vernon spoke into the ear piece. Tony looked down at the table a moment and excused himself again.

"You got something?" he said as he opened the door.

Vernon pointed to me and shrugged.

"Ask him if his grandmother killed Patel."

Tony and Vernon froze. "Luanne, I..." Tony looked to Vernon for help.

"Ask him," said Vernon and shrugged again.

Watching a burly man, who makes his living fighting with rig-ging on boats, break down and cry, is a miserable sight. Corwin held it in as long as possible. When it came, it burst like a pent up volcano.

"Yes!" He clamped his hands against his cheeks and stammered through loud sobs. "I've worked and worked and worked. Even after all the others left. After the wives left. Aaron and I stuck around and cared for that woman. We were making it finally." He took one fist and pounded the table top until his lawyer reached over and pushed his hand down. I half expected that fist to rise up and flatten the attorney's face. Instead, Corwin stretched his fingers as though he wanted them to pop off. A uniformed deputy entered the room, standing at the door in case of real violence.

Corwin's grief and anger took hold of the man's body and he shook as though in a terrible chill. He finally jerked off the prison shirt and used it as a towel for his face.

"Tell me how she did it," Tony said in a measured voice, his eyes darting once toward the two-way mirror.

The lawyer stood now, staring down at his client, occasionally leaning against the wall.

"We saw her!" Corwin lifted the shirt from his face. His eyes and skin were the same color. Sweat poured off his forehead and mixed with the tears. "I was standing there on the other side, the swimming side of the lake. Me and Trukee were arguing. He wanted to borrow money to buy that boat, but I didn't think he'd ever make enough to pay it back." Corwin hiccuped and laughed. "He didn't know a damn thing about the illegals. Had no idea what we were doing. You won't get him on that."

"But he saw your grandmother, too?"

"We were standing there. He stopped talking about money and said 'what the hell is your grandma doing?'" We watched as she came out the kitchen door and walked on her tiptoes like she was inside a hallway. She had something in her hand, but she was too far away. I think I complained about taking care of a senile old lady or something like that, when she turned to her right and went under the oak tree limbs from the other side.

He gulped and the tears started streaming again.

"Somebody, a man, yelled from under that tree. 'Woman, what are you doing?'" He hit the table again. "It was Patel's voice. We both knew the accent. He half stumbled from the tree. That's when she…" Corwin closed his eyes. "She came out and hit him right in the neck. I didn't know how but blood spurted everywhere. Patel grabbed his neck but the blood kept spurting until he fell on the ground and trembled. Like when someone dies. She tossed the weapon on top of him and turned around and ran to the hose up against the house. She put that hose on top of her head and literally showered off. Took all signs of blood off her hands, her clothes, her face, her hair." Corwin dropped his head to the table and wept. Tony and the lawyer waited for him to recover.

"Trukee and I ran over to the man, but he was dead. At least we could feel no pulse."

"And what did you do then?"

"We thought about putting him in the sinkhole, but there had been too much activity around it lately. That's when Trukee suggested putting him on the shrimp boat and dumping him to the gators in the river." He smiled. "Said he'd help and keep his mouth shut if I'd buy the boat for him. Did I have a choice? We got an old tarp, pulled off his clothes, rolled him up and put him on the boat as soon as I came up the river with the delivery."

"Where did you keep him between the time he died and when you put him on the boat?"

"Just wrapped him in the tarp and stashed him under that tree. Nobody goes under it anymore. The branches are too low."

"Patel went under it, and evidently, so did your grandmother."

"I don't know how she knew he was there." He frowned and wiped his face with his shirt.

"We'll have to ask her, you know." Tony shifted in his chair.

"Do you have any idea why your grandmother would want to kill the man?"

"She's crazy, that's all." Corwin looked into Tony's face. "Was Patel on to us?"

"Big time," said Tony. He nodded for the attorney to sit down again. "Let's wrap this up. You and Trukee got the body on the boat. He went off with the clothes and burned them. You dumped the body in the river. What did you do with the tarp?"

"I gave it to Trukee to burn the next day. He really liked that little oyster boat."

"You used barbed wire to hold him down?"

Corwin squeezed his eyes shut. "That was a fiasco. We were afraid the body would surface. I had some old wire and tried wrapping it around a cement block. The wire broke before we ever got him off the boat. Too rusted." Corwin shook his head, staring ahead until his eyes watered. He looked the completely defeated man.

"And the oyster knife, you chunked it overboard with the body?"

Corwin smiled again. "I'd forgotten about it. I had tossed it in the tarp with the man and when I rolled him into the water, it went with him." He swiped his face with the shirt, now looking like a dirty rag. "Do you have any idea what it's like to see your own grandmother kill a man?" He shook his head without stopping. "She got us into such a mess with that one act."

"Tell me," said Tony. "What would you have done about the incident if you hadn't been transporting illegals?"

Corwin stopped for several moments, then let out a puff of air. "Reported her to you guys and had her committed."

We sat in the observation room in silence long after Corwin was led back to his cell.

"I don't think I've ever investigated a crazy old lady who has killed a police informant," said Tony. "We'll have to pick her up."

"What will happen to her?" I said. I knew it would be an institution eventually, but the thought of this old lady in a jail full of screaming inmates seemed wrong.

"She'll stay in the hospital ward in the jail until the judge rules on her condition. It won't take long. No one wants to see her stranded here."

Shoulders drooped. It was after midnight. Sissy would be snuggled on a couch in a house with her great-grandmother for the last time.

"Will you see Corwin again soon?" I asked Tony.

"Soon as we get something ready for him to sign in the way of a statement. Maybe tonight."

I pulled the orange from my pocket and placed it in his hand. "Could you give this to him? His daughter, Sissy, sent it."

CHAPTER TWENTY-TWO

"How did you know Tony should ask about the grandmother?" said Vernon. He sat beside me in the Honda, one hand ruffling my hair, the other holding onto his bandaged middle in expectation of road bumps.

"I'll show you, or let you hear, why when we get home. Iris Henderson made some tapes of Beatrice talking about the legend of her husband. She said something that could have been the ramblings of senility, but it didn't quite strike me that way."

"One crazy female knows another," he said. "Tony won't sleep for a week. He hates it when you do that."

"No, he doesn't. He loves it. He mostly gets the credit for solving anything just by being the lead detective." I pretended to hit him in the stomach. "Besides, I can't help it if he hasn't evolved far enough to have intuition."

Before we reached my swamp road, Vernon got a call from Tony. They would pick Beatrice up first thing in the morning. He wanted me to be there. "He expects emotion," said Vernon.

"Sissy isn't going to let that old woman go without an argument." I dreaded the intrusion in their lives. The kid had worked hard to keep the woman in her own house. All that tending to boarders and grabbing what she could to eat for Beatrice as well as herself. Not to mention taking a homemade boat to her cousin's for schooling. "She thought she was doing the right thing by dealing with the day-to-day drudgery. No one at that house seems to have had any real beauty in their lives." I turned to see Vernon watching me.

"You don't plan to take her in your house, do you?" He wasn't smiling. Our lives had been free, outside of the constraints of marriage bonds and children. Sissy in the house would certainly change that.

I sighed. "Why do I feel obligated? But, no, I don't have the need for a child, no matter what Pasquin has in mind for my life plan. She's going to be a teen soon, a handful for sure. It will have to be Rachel, of course. She's the only relative and the court will deem her responsible. She won't like it much, but she'll do it."

"Guilt has made more than one mother," said Vernon.

I shook my head but couldn't think of another thing to say.

"I'm going to call Iris to help out tomorrow," I said. "She'll be shocked but pleased to be a part of this."

We sat on the bed and listened to Beatrice's CD. Vernon had me play the part about the brown and white arms twice.

"She saw Patel's arms from her window," I said, "and got them confused with her husband's arms from long ago."

"Why would she want to kill her husband, if that's what she thought she was doing?"

"I don't know. Sissy said she nearly tore his desk apart when she found it in the attic. Burned all his papers she found there, too. She's still angry after fifty years."

"Would have been nice to see what was in that desk."

We slept in each other's arms, sort of. His middle was too sore for me to hold him tight. It was more like a gentle laying on of hands.

Before dawn a clatter rose from the direction of the river. It was as though someone couldn't find a radio station and kept going from one loud station to another.

"What the hell!" said Vernon. He tried to roll out of bed and take the stairs two at a time. His sore body rebelled and he sat down on the top step. "That's a new noise." He pointed toward the river.

I staggered downstairs. I knew it was that Holy Roller boat, its microphone gone crazy. Why was it on the river at this time of morning? I grabbed a sweat shirt and pulled it over my pajamas. The moisture in the air sat as a heavy fog over the land and water. Heading for the landing, I heard Plato running up the path, barking at the devil.

The converted tour boat had stopped near my dock and listed to one side. Someone on board kept slapping and banging at a machine.

"What do you think you're doing?" I yelled. The boat was maybe fifteen feet from the landing.

"Damn thing broke down, and I can't get this speaker hookup to work." The man talking shoved his white hair upward, where it stayed even in the mist. "I'll get it in a minute."

"You're not planning on preaching at this hour?"

He looked up at me, his blue eyes round and fearful. "Why not?"

"Because you and God are going to get arrested if you do! There's a deputy sheriff right in that house who is annoyed with your disturbance."

He looked toward the house and stepped back from the knob he was turning. "Oh."

"If you need help, I'll call someone, but you keep that microphone and speaker turned off. Clear?"

He bobbed his head and attempted to turn on the motor. It worked after a few tries, and he guided it toward the center of the river. The last I saw was the "Jesus Saves" sign fading into the fog. "I wonder if he's a member of the Moon family," I said to Plato.

Inside, Vernon called his office and made arrangements for someone to give the man a stern warning about using a microphone up and down the river. "Man is a religious disturbance," he said.

I dreaded the morning that was coming through the fog. Sissy would have to watch her great-grandmother go away with people in uniforms, probably never to see her Moon Island house again.

"How much can a twelve-year-old take?" I asked Vernon as we rode to Fogarty Spring. Tony wanted me there to hold Sissy's hand and convince her that Beatrice had to go with them. In my head, it wasn't only Sissy's hand that would need holding. I'd practically have to tie her down when she found out about Patel.

"Children can bounce back," said Vernon. "If she gets in the right place and has some guidance. I doubt she's had any to this point."

We parked next to Rachel's house. Tony's unmarked car was down the street, and a well-marked patrol car sat across the street.

I knocked on the door. Sissy answered it, dressed with recently combed hair.

"I know why you're here," she said. Her face seemed resigned, almost relieved. "I saw that patrol car across the street. I got myself ready and then told Grandma to get up. She's quiet today. I had to dress her, but she's had some hot water and cereal."

Vernon and I looked at each other. How could she have known?

"What do you know?" he asked.

"They're going to take Grandma to jail for killing Patel, aren't they?"

I sat on the couch. "Sissy, how in the world…?"

"Somebody called here and told me. I won't say who. I didn't tell Rachel. She's still asleep." She pointed toward the bedrooms down the hall. "I gave Grandma a tranquilizer. She won't holler or nothing."

Vernon went outside and talked to Tony. When they came in, they had a uniformed deputy and a nurse in white slacks and jacket with them.

Sissy got up, her troubles pressing, went into the back room and brought Mrs. Moon to the uniformed deputy. She let go of the woman's hand and placed it in the nurse's hand.

"She won't understand anything you say to her." Sissy shrugged and sat on the couch.

Tony recited the rights in a low voice, knowing full well it wouldn't count for anything. Mrs. Moon's eyes were blank, looking at something far beyond what was happening in this house.

"She'll be fine," the nurse said to Sissy. "We'll let you know how things are." She took Beatrice's arm and led her to the car. There was no resistance.

The room remained quiet. Vernon sat on a chair and glanced at me once in a while. I had an arm around Sissy's shoulder but she pushed it away. Not in anger, but maybe because she just didn't want to bear the burden of anything there anymore.

"Do you want to stay here?" I asked.

Sissy shook her head and looked at her shoes. No bare feet this morning. "I want to go somewhere away from this swamp. I'd like to live in a city." She jerked her head up and looked at Vernon. "Is it possible to change my name?"

Vernon looked startled. "Yes, I think so. We can look into it if you want." He turned to me for help.

"Sissy, you don't want to live with a foster family, do you?"

"Anything would be better than living on that island."

Before we could go any further, a door slammed open and Rachel pranced into view, her nightgown clinging to her ample body and her hair frizzed about her head.

"What in the world?"

"You missed it all, Rachel," I said.

Vernon stood and held his hand out to Sissy. "Let's take a walk, okay. Maybe have some crab cakes at Mama's Table."

She stood and took his hand. "I'd rather have bacon and eggs, thank you."

Rachel stood at the door. Without the touches of make-up and lavender water or whatever she normally used, she looked a mess. Her body smelled of night sweats.

"You didn't hear when they took Beatrice away?"

"What?" She gasped and placed one hand across her chest. Without her bra, she seemed just one full bag of flesh. "I took a sleeping pill. I don't hear anything when I have one of those."

"She murdered one of her boarders," I said. "She'll end up in an institution. They couldn't let her stay free."

Rachel stared at me for a long time, her eyes opened in horror. "Who?"

I sat her at the table and poured her what was left of the hot water Sissy had made for Beatrice. Rachel dipped a tea bag in it.

"Tell me, did someone call here last night and speak to Sissy?"

"Yes. Corwin did. They let him call from jail. She said he wanted to thank her for an orange she sent him."

I smiled. "He probably did that, too. I'll bet he told her a few other things. She knew the deputies would be here this morning."

"Why didn't she tell me!" She had been affronted, taken for granted by this family that she half loathed. "The little brat."

"No, no, Rachel. Don't call her that. She's been something

akin to Florence Nightingale for too long. Look at her age. Has she had a childhood?"

"Has anyone?" She rose in anger, taking her coffee cup to the window to see if anyone was watching.

I couldn't answer her question. I didn't even know why it was asked. Instead, I looked at her standing there in the morning light, her lumpy body outlined beneath her gown, her frizzy hair flying about the ears and across her back. Her bare feet were swollen, both had bunions. This was a far cry from the preening bathing beauty that starred in her own little drama before the eyes of fishermen. That wasn't a wise thing to do, I thought. Many of these men had been on open ocean for days with only each other for company.

"I'm going to have to call your professor friend," she said as she turned back to me. "She was coming today for more recording. I couldn't."

"Wait. Why not let this be the day she records Sissy? She wants to, you know. I can arrange to have her do it somewhere else."

"Good! Do that." Rachel paced the floor and cursed when she realized there was no more hot water. She took her cup to the kitchen and filled a tea kettle with more. "I can't, you see, just can't take on the raising of that child. I don't mind making decisions about her schooling and such, but we must find another place for her to live."

I leaned on the wall next to the kitchen door. "Rachel, I doubt the courts will let you make decisions for her if you don't take her into your guardianship."

She gave me a stern look but said nothing and turned back to her tea..

I picked up the phone to call Iris.

"Do you think she'll talk to me after something so awful?" Iris had listened as I told her in a low voice that Beatrice's days of freedom were done. "Dear me, murder. How can the child take that?"

"She's taken a lot over the years. That's why I think it might be good for her to tell the legend as she knows it. But, Rachel doesn't want it done here. You can use my living room while I'm at the university."

"No. I have a better idea. Bring her to school with you today. I'll pick her up and take her to my place. We might even go out for lunch. She doesn't eat often at restaurants, right?"

"Try never," I said. I agreed. Maybe Sissy would appreciate a day out of this swamp.

"Thanks for getting her out of the house," said Rachel who sat at the table again. She had made some toast and slapped it with butter and jelly. "That old lady Moon was always a pain for us all. Thank goodness she's no real blood kin to me."

"Her children and grandchildren are kin to you," I said. "But maybe they took after Mr. Moon instead of her." I was trying to be facetious, to more or less mock her heritage.

"Mr. Moon," Rachel said and nodded.

I turned away. The one hope was Sissy. She had a father, an uncle, and now a great-grandmother in jail, not to mention a cousin who wanted nothing to do with her.

"I'll be in touch, Rachel. You'll need to know what's happening with the family." I walked out the door and headed for Mama's Table.

"I'm going to town?" Sissy's eyes glowed. "Can I stay overnight?"

"I doubt that, but you'll be there all day. You know what Professor Henderson does, don't you?"

She nodded. "Studies the way people talk. I'll talk for her." She

finished the bacon omelet on her plate and drank all of the orange juice.

"Sounds like a good deal," said Vernon who nursed his coffee.

All the way into town, Sissy asked us questions about Iris' house,
what was it like, did she have neighbors, did she live alone, did she
let children play inside? I answered what I knew. What I really did
was stifle my own questions about Beatrice's motive for killing
Patel. I was sure there was one even if it was embedded inside the
woman's confused brain. I didn't realize people with senility could
actually murder, but what did I know?

Iris was sitting in the department office when I arrived. We ran
late because I had to drop off Vernon at the sheriff's office. I led
Sissy and Iris to chairs in my office and I hurried to class.

What happened during the hour I was gone must have been a
miracle. Sissy's face beamed when I plopped my notes on my office desk.

"We're going to watch a DVD," she said. "Iris has the Harry
Potter movies."

I stopped to remind myself that this child had no television.
Any movie she saw would be an occasional outing with a friend
or maybe with Rachel's class. She lived with an old woman who
wouldn't let her go swimming. And with a father whom she ad-
dressed by his first name. Seeing a DVD movie inside a well-
furnished house where there was plenty of food and a woman
who wanted to listen to you talk, it had to be a born again experience.

I told Tony where Sissy would be. Children's Services had no
objection because Iris was a teacher like Rachel and a similar age.
The two of them left the building together, chatting away about
places where they could eat.

The world inside my classroom was indeed different from the

swamp world where I lived. It never occurred to me that the one that crowded people into plastic desks and vied for parking spaces would be more alive than a frog chorus or a battle between an alligator and a young deer. Sissy saw it that way. Her world was a fight for survival with the constant reminder of ravages of old age and the troubles of traumatized minds. She wanted the city, the bustle with gas fumes in the air and bumping shopping carts.

I phoned Tony as soon as my class ended.

"What will happen to the house on Moon Island," I asked. "Will the property go to Sissy?"

"Whatever is left, if anything. Most likely, it will be sold and the profits used to defend the brothers, house Beatrice in a nursing home, and pay support for Sissy until she's eighteen. We'll have to ask some lawyers. Might be something leftover in the land. Put it this way, she'll probably be the heir if anything is left over. Unless, of course, any of the ones who left try to lay claim."

"Surely, Tony, they wouldn't turn it over to one of those relatives."

"I'm not an expert there, Luanne. Talk to the attorneys. Doubt they'll tell you anything right now. As for me, I've got the search warrant and we're on our way there in an hour."

"I'd give anything to be a fly on that wall," I said.

"You won't be. You've got conflicting interests in this one."

CHAPTER TWENTY-THREE

Sissy stayed with Iris. When she phoned and said she'd be spending the night, I offered to pick up her things at Rachel's and bring them.

"Not tonight. Iris has bought me some pajamas and a pair of jeans and a tee-shirt."

She sounded so up that I forced myself not to worry. To my knowledge, Iris had always been kind, and she sure was smart. That couldn't hurt Sissy.

"Maybe I see her slipping away from me," I said to Pasquin as we rocked in the twilight, a custom that never changed over the years. "She wanted to learn to swim and dive and she was doing well."

"Quit moaning, ma'am. You didn't want the responsibility of a child."

"It's not the child so much as the friend."

Pasquin pushed his head against the high back of the rocking chair. "She'll get back to it. You got to give her space right now. She's used to dealing with old ladies, and Iris Henderson is finally a sane one. Good for her."

"You're right," I said and reached over to pat his arm.

"She ought not to be with Rachel anyhow. That was a wild

one."

"What makes you say that? She seems like the old school marm to me."

He laughed low in his throat. "She is now. But her body was important to her according to Gavi. He told me a little more about her over the bourbon bottle last night."

"He's here?"

"Was here. He's looking for some young men to help him work on that falling down cabin of his. Edwin will go for a while."

"Edwin? I guess he could clear the area of snakes. Like a Saint Edwin," I laughed. "You know, Saint Patrick—Saint Edwin."

"I'm Catholic, Luanne. I know my saints." He let loose with a loud laugh, "And Edwin ain't one of them. Can't you see Saint Patrick taking all those Irish snakes and hauling them back to his monastery, puttin' them in cages, and making belts for the monk's robes."

"Saint Edwin will. If you can call his swamp house a monastery."

We rocked and listened to the sounds of approaching night in the forest. A boat moved upriver, returning from a long day of fishing on the Gulf. The pilot saw our one little light burning on the porch and pulled his horn in salute.

"That image of a young Rachel parading around in her bathing suit just for men like that boatman to ogle at her is almost haunting."

"Haunting. More like arousing."

"No. Haunting when you look at her now. She liked men, or at least liked that they admired her, but she never married. Come to think of it, none of the stories she tells even mentions a boyfriend."

"Bet she had one." Pasquin nodded, his white hair the only

thing visible in the weak light. "Standing out there in a tight yellow suit, long red hair, long smooth white legs and arms. She knew what she was doing."

The image was a pretty one, at least as far as Rachel went. The fair skin with the red hair and perfect figure. She would have been desirable to any man, young and old.

"Why do you suppose she never married?"

Pasquin turned toward me. "You didn't."

"Sigh! I guess I was just doomed to be a spinster." I grabbed his hat and gave him a slap on the hand. "I never paraded myself around like a bathing beauty, letting men gawk at me."

"She came of age just before the sixties. Isn't that when women started saying to hell with the rules, burned their bras, and refused to be sex objects."

"Later in the sixties. In 1959, girls still wanted boys to marry them and make them happy for sixty-five years."

"Guess she went to college instead."

"No. You got the time wrong. She went to college, yes, but that's where lots of women found their husbands. She didn't." I threw my hands in the air. "Why am I arguing about this? The woman decided not to marry. That's all."

"Didn't she say she never went back to the Moon house after that summer when the old man went into the lake?"

"Yes. It would have been traumatic, and not something she'd want to think about when she was swimming underwater."

"Boats with fishermen still tied up there."

Darkness enclosed us. Pasquin decided he needed to go home and headed for the landing. He often walked the swamp path in the dark, but tonight, he'd have the safety of the river.

"If you see the old hound dog, tell him his supper is waiting."

I sat for awhile on the porch. Plato did come in from some

dark corner he had been exploring. A boat went by, its fishermen whooping and hollering over some dirty joke. Days must have been long on that ocean and the cover of night with the rigging folded brought out male camaraderie. If they took off upriver and headed for one of the juke joints, they could ogle at pretty girls in skimpy blouses and tight jeans.

"Only now they don't settle for just ogling," I said.

I lay awake in bed for nearly two hours, seeing Rachel come out from under that tree. In my mind, she passed for a Marilyn Monroe-Maureen O'Hara combo. A young Gavi would be sitting on the deck of his shrimp boat, a little hidden behind a rigging perhaps. His fantasies would carry him through the next few hours of hot and dangerous toil on the sea.

At seven, I awoke with a start. There was no noise in the house. Plato wasn't begging to go outside. And there was no Holy Roller blasting nonsense about my sins. Something in my head triggered the reaction. Brown arms, white arms. I got dressed, sipped on a strong cup of coffee and made a phone call.

"I need to pick up some things for Sissy," I said. "I'll bring some nice rolls and we can talk."

On the way to Rachel's house, I took some deep breaths. I could be terribly wrong. I parked near Mama's Table and went inside to buy some of the cheese rolls that she handed out with big Southern breakfasts. They weren't Southern, but Danish sweet things. She had no qualms about adding them to the menu. They were too good to be avoided just because they originated in a cold, northern country. "And give me two large coffees," I said, not knowing if Rachel would be willing to make it.

She was dressed today, an improvement over the nightgown, but the skin below her eyes sagged and appeared dark. She hadn't slept well. Her hair, once long and flowing in natural curls, was dampened with some kind of gel and twisted in a bun on top of her head.

"I put her things in a bag," she said. "The sheriff said I'm to leave Beatrice's things just where they are. They'll want to go through them later." She pulled off the lid of the take-out coffee and slipped a roll from the box. "Have they found the weapon yet?"

"Oh yes. They have all they need."

"And will Dr. Henderson be back to record me?"

"I'm not sure." This surprised me. "Do you want her to come back?"

"I was beginning to enjoy it. She said if she wrote an article, my name might be mentioned as a source."

"You're used to attention, aren't you?" I smiled, hoping she'd take it as a compliment.

"In my day!" She took a big bite of the sweet roll.

"You must have been a desirable young lady. Long red hair, great shape."

"It happened once upon a time."

"But you tossed it all away to be an unmarried teacher. Surely you could have done both."

"You're not married." She had stopped eating and glared at me.

"I'm another generation. And I'm not even half as pretty as you were."

She didn't question how I knew this. Flattery still worked on her, and she smiled in a coy way that might have charmed some young oyster shucker right off the dock.

"I know the Moon boys were your cousins, but I'll bet they flirted with you, or at least told their friends about their pretty relative."

She blushed now, and shrugged her shoulders. "Yes, I think they did."

"And if old man Moon was anything like Pasquin is now, he'd tease you something awful about boys coming to court."

She fidgeted with her roll and coffee, dropping some of both on her chest.

"He didn't like boys sniffing around me."

"And his wife?"

She shoved the chair back. "That old bitty—and she was old even then. She'd watch everything from her window. She'd try and hide behind the curtains, but I'd see them move and her shadow move across."

"Is that why you spent time beneath the big oak limbs, to try and stay out of her vision?"

"That was one reason, yes. I mean what was wrong with a girl wanting to go for a swim? I didn't swim with the boys. I honored her wishes on that one."

"He didn't want you to swim with them, either, did he?"

She stood up, her hands on her hips. "No."

"Rachel, why didn't you ever marry?" I watched her walk toward a window and come back again.

"The sins one commits as a youth aren't carried into adulthood, are they?"

I shrugged. "We all make our beds and pay in our own ways."

"My mother was almost as strict as Beatrice, you know. As was my father. They ground it into my brain that I was to never let a boy touch me, that I had to be a virgin when I married. If I wasn't, my husband would know and wouldn't ever like me much after that, might even divorce me. A virgin, imagine that." She gave a sneering laugh and stood with her face to the wall. "That old man made sure I wasn't one."

I froze. I had expected a young cousin, even Gavi, or one of the others, even a rape with a bunch of sailors, but this made sense.

"Two summers in a row. He took every advantage as they say. I think Beatrice knew something was happening, but she just watched from her window. Maybe she hoped she'd catch him."

"You were willing?"

She turned suddenly, her eyes blazing. "Of course, not! I couldn't stand the old man. I wanted a young man, my age, but he's what I got until…" She stopped abruptly and faced the wall again.

"You pushed him into that lake, didn't you? You used your pretty white arms and pushed him from under the tree branches right into the lake."

She said nothing.

"He could swim and shout. Why didn't he? Perhaps he was silenced first, then pushed in, right?" I was taking a chance on going too far, but once a confession begins, it's often finished.

Beatrice turned around again and marched into the kitchen. She returned with a bottle of rum and unscrewed the top. Taking a long swig right from the bottle, she sat down hard and faced me.

"He'd been at me twice that day, and he wanted something to happen right out there at the lake. Wanted me to take off my bathing suit and lie under that tree. I'd had enough." She closed her eyes and took another drink. She began talking in a whisper. "There was a board under that tree, the seat to an old swing that had rotted down. I waited until he stooped over to untie his shoes. The board was heavy but my young arms lifted it with ease and let it down on the back of his head. He didn't pass out, just staggered away from the tree toward the water. I took a chance and pushed him. He fell hard into that lake. I stood back and waited for him to come up, but he never did. A shrimper had tied up, and I knew he'd be watching for me. I don't know how, but I came out and dived into that water. I swam underneath, looking out for a body but never seeing one. I came up on the other side, and two men applauded when I got out."

I stared at her. She had pushed the old man into the lake in 1959. A lake that is really a sinkhole. He went down and probably got caught on something that kept him there. He might have been dazed from the board over the head. Whatever the reason, he didn't have the strength to rise to the surface. And the watching fishermen applauded her graceful swim. That would have mattered more than they knew.

"And, Miss Fogarty, I was no longer a virgin. That's why I never married." She spit the "Miss" at me.

"I see." I leaned back. "You need to tell the sheriff. You had a right to defend yourself, and you were a juvenile."

She said nothing, but slung her head back and guzzled the rum. I tried to pull it away, but she jerked herself from the table and drank again. When she fell on the couch in a stupor, I phoned Tony.

"Beatrice got her time line mixed up, combined the past and present to come up with arms—brown and white ones." I stood talking with Tony after the deputies had escorted Rachel to a car and drove her to be booked. "She stood at that bedroom window in 1959 and saw white arms—Rachel's pretty white arms—dart out and shove her husband into the water. Somewhere in that brain of hers, she changed it to him walking into the water. Maybe she was afraid to tell what she knew he'd been doing."

"And Patel happened to be standing in just the right place," said Tony.

"Yes. He was watching and listening to Corwin and Trukee.

Trying to catch information about illegals. He must have exposed his arms at some point and that action triggered something in her demented mind. She was watching out the window in 1959 all over again. Who knows what she was thinking when she took the oyster knife and sneaked down to the tree."

Tony sighed. "That's just speculation, Luanne."

"True, we don't know. But it spurred something in my head."

He looked at me and half smiled. "Don't you have a class to teach?"

"It's Saturday."

CHAPTER TWENTY-FOUR

We sat underwater and watched a turtle swim above us. Behind it, three baby turtles swam in a straight line. It would head for a sunny log and rest there, the three babies basking with it, still in a straight line. Sissy nodded behind the mask. Her bubbles made a trail to the surface like the bubbles of joy inside her. She was learning to use the underwater breathing device. Had I left her to her own whims, she would have headed for the deep river section to find the small cave off my landing.

"Diving is dangerous," I had told her. "You must have the knowledge of the systems you're using as well as the body of water you choose to invade. Otherwise, you may not live to see your second set of fins."

She laughed at me, but agreed. I had never seen Sissy laugh until she settled in with Iris. It was like both gave each other life. Iris reveled in a young pupil who listened as she explained the phonetic concepts of the Moon accent, and the possibilities of how the odd past tense evolved. Sissy was a quick student who adored Iris, not only grateful for shelter and schooling in a place with brick walls and classmates, but for encouraging her every whim to know things.

I knew I'd made the right choice when I suggested Iris. Something in me had been selfish, wanting to keep the kid for the daughter I'd never have. Iris, ever the emeritus professor, made the logical argument.

"Let me be the one who takes care of her on a daily basis, the one who schools her, and teaches her the right way to act in company," said Iris. "You can be her godmother, the one responsible if I become incapacitated, and the one who teaches her to dive and deal with the swamps."

Vernon sighed when he heard me agree. In spite of his calm exterior, he sounded jealous when he pointed out how hard it would be to wander the halls in the nude, how sound carried in my old house. "We'd have to tippy-toe through everything," he said. "A third person makes a huge difference."

"Maybe a second person in Iris' house is what she needs," I said. "Sissy likes being with her."

"Yes, and she's pretty good at following through with things. She won't neglect the kid."

"Except she never did find out what the emergency was in 1985 that kept her from studying the island, but she didn't have to," I said. "I figured it out myself. Hurricane Kate came through in November that year. That old house and the island must have taken a beating."

"To tell you the truth," Vernon said, "the fact that the old house withstood those winds is proof of its solid bones."

And that's the way it stood. Sissy went to live with Iris.

"Iris bought me some fins and a mask," she said one day. "She'll buy me a scuba tank, too. But I have to learn it first."

My Saturday mornings belonged to Sissy now. Iris brought her and sometimes waited on the porch for the lessons to finish. Most of the time, however, she struck out somewhere to listen to the locals. This morning, she had arranged to record Edwin on his landing. It wasn't much to sit on, but Iris wasn't about to go into that yard again. She had laughed when we called him the snake man of the swamp. After venturing there with Pasquin only one time, she fled and wouldn't move past the dock again. Edwin set up lawn chairs and turned over a crate for a table. Pasquin often went with her and sat in Edwin's little boat, his hat over his face. To get Edwin to talk, she had to listen to snake stories. The tape was peppered with background chuckles as Pasquin sensed Iris' unease when a diamond back rattler appeared beneath a porch when Edwin was only six or when he watched a cotton mouth drop from an overhanging limb into a rowboat.

Sissy and I rested on my landing. She owned her own bathing suit now.

"I hear a car," she said. She had a great ear, one that listened for extraordinary things. A car engine wasn't the same as a cicada chorus or panther cry.

Sure enough, Tony's unmarked car came down the road and parked right in front of my steps. He was with Vernon.

"Two bathing beauties," said Vernon, without thinking. I had asked him not to tease Sissy when she was in a bathing suit. It brought back too many memories of how Rachel played that game in her youth.

"Two divers," I said. "She's getting the hang of it."

Sissy tossed me a towel and we joined them on the porch. For Tony to be out here couldn't be a social visit.

"I've got some things for you, Sissy. They came from the house on Moon Island. They've been sorted through and boxed. Nothing there we can use. I guess you know the docs have been conducting their psychiatric evaluations these past six weeks. The judge will make a final ruling tomorrow."

"Will they send her to the crazy house?" said Sissy.

Tony looked at me, surprised that Sissy would ask.

"I don't know exactly what the judge will say, but most likely he's going to order a permanent residence in her current facility." Tony wouldn't look at the girl.

"The crazy house," said Sissy. "She'll be happy there."

"Why do you say that?" asked Vernon. He had come to treat her almost as an adult and found it got a better response from her.

"That place where she is… it's a great big old white house. She's on the third floor with a big window. There's a holding pond on the next lot, with lots of trees around it. The last time I was there, she had her chair next to that window and just stared down at the pond and the trees. She wouldn't speak, but I knew she was thinking of Oscar walking into the water."

Sissy had begun using first names to speak of her great-grandmother and her husband. Remarkably, Corwin had become Pops. He told her on one visit that he'd always wanted to be called Pops, and she went along with it now. In a twisted way, she had a renewed respect for her father.

"Is Trukee still at the house?" she asked.

Tony nodded. "Charges were dropped after he agreed to cooperate with the Feds. He'll face a charge for helping remove Patel's body, but he won't do much time." He looked at Sissy. "He loves that oyster boat. Seems to be making a living off it."

"Even if it was bought with dirty money," said Vernon.

"Pops will get jail time, won't he?" Sissy's face turned sour.

"For transporting illegals, most likely. For concealing a body, not too much." Uncomfortable with too much emotional talk, Tony slapped his knee and said, "Where do you want me to put those boxes?"

We finally decided to store them on my front porch until we could get them to Iris' house. Vernon, his bruised midsection healed now, helped Tony stack them.

"This one has some nice old photos," Vernon said. "If you like that sort of thing."

Sissy ran inside for a felt pen. She wrote PHOTOS on one side. "I want to look at these things," she said. "I want to see what these people looked like when all this stuff happened."

I walked with Vernon to the car. Sissy was already opening the box on the porch.

"It's good for her," I said. "She'll make some sense out of things when she sees people who look right for the part. Two old ladies who hate and murder, it's miscast."

"She's lucky to have another nutty old lady who will help her. What's the latest on that?"

"Iris? Unless they find some other relatives wanting and able to care for her, which I doubt, the courts will let her legally keep her." I poked him. "Especially if people in law enforcement recommend it."

Tony and Vernon left us to our forest primeval. Their car had silenced all the frogs for the moment, but a woodpecker hacked away at the bark of a tall pine somewhere back in the woods. Life has its way of going on, of ignoring past disturbances. Did we learn from them?

Sissy and I sat on our towels on the porch boards and went through the pictures. Most were in black and white, some even in sepia tones, but a few were in faded colors like the ones of Rachel in her yellow bathing suit.

"No wonder the boys stared at her," I said. "She was a beauty for that time."

Sissy turned up her nose. "She's pudgy."

"Not for that time," I said. "She would have been called voluptuous. Lots of chest," I used my hands to suggest large breasts.

"And her muscles have no tone."

"Toned muscles would probably have been considered too masculine for the time." I had to smile. Sissy was entering her teens, the age when one's body means just about everything.

She tossed the photos on the pile, careful to keep them in the same arrangement we found them. There were several more of a posing Rachel, all in the same suit, some near the infamous oak tree.

"Here's the whole group," Sissy said, holding one picture with both hands. She passed it to me and moved to look over my shoulder.

"Beatrice, for sure!" I pointed to a young woman who might have been pretty if not for the scowl. Her eyebrows pressed a line in her brow and her down turned mouth barely showed her lips.

"She didn't say cheese," Sissy laughed.

"And I know why." I pointed to the girl beside her. She seemed a younger version of the Rachel we saw in the bathing suit. Not quite as developed, but still cute as a button with long curly hair pulled back with barrettes. She smiled and held the hand of a dashing man who could have been in his late forties, early fifties.

"That's Oscar, I'll bet," said Sissy.

We both stared in silence. The man was gorgeous, handsome in those days, with a full head of hair graying on the sides. He was tall with a build that looked like he worked out, but maybe he just worked hard. Instead of wearing his shirt, he appeared to be carrying it over one shoulder.

I had plenty to say about this man who looked like he could have had any woman in the county, but picked a child, but I kept my mouth shut. Sissy did the same. Whatever went on in her head about the role her great-grandfather played in the family ruin would stay there.

Before we could each get lost in our own angst over the un-
fairness of the Moon family fate, a noise like guitars and drums
sounded from down the river. Coming closer, we put everything
away and watched an old tour boat with a speaker system chug
upriver. Three men sat in the open window seats. They each played
an instrument, electric guitar, banjo, and drums. The microphone
stood so that each could yell out a country song. As it passed us,
I saw the side where "Jesus Saves" had been painted over in a thin
layer of white. Someone had tacked a sign in its place: "Band For
Hire. Make Your Next Party a Wild One."

We looked at each other. "Jesus didn't save that one," I said.
We both laughed hard and long.

"Let's go back in the river," Sissy shouted and took off down
the ladder into the water.

She turned toward me and raised a hand then pointed to a tree
trunk that had fallen into the spring long ago. A school of bream
swam up to the log and scooted over it, their tiny bodies trem-
bling like children on a playground.

Over the next few months, I watched this pupil of mine learn to
swim and dive and use the water for refuge from pain. Whatever
the members of her family had done to lose the homestead that
she should have inherited didn't matter at all when she could drift
along silently with fish and snails for company. Her universe of
face mask, scuba tank, and fins allowed her to escape into a universe that made sense, where animals followed instinct, and the
aquifers shot out pristine water as cold as ice.

Recommended Memento Mori Mysteries

Viv Powers Mysteries by Letha Albright
DAREDEVIL'S APPRENTICE
BAD-LUCK WOMAN

A Katlin LaMar Mystery by Sherri L. Board
BLIND BELIEF

Matty Madrid Mysteries by P.J. Grady
MAXIMUM INSECURITY
DEADLY SIN

A Dr. Rebecca Temple Mystery
by Sylvia Maultash Warsh
TO DIE IN SPRING

AN UNCERTAIN CURRENCY
Clyde Lynwood Sawyer, Jr.
Frances Witlin

A Suzanne LaFleshe Mystery by Hollis Seamon
FLESH

THE COLOR OF EMPTINESS
a crime novel by Cynthia Webb

Other books by Glynn Marsh Alam:

RIVER WHISPERS

Luanne Fogarty Mysteries
DIVE DEEP and DEADLY
DEEP WATER DEATH
COLD WATER CORPSE
BILGE WATER BONES
HIGH WATER HELLION
GREEN WATER GHOST

Glynn Marsh Alam is a native Floridian. Born in Tallahassee, she is familiar with the live oak forests and cypress swamps of the area. She also knows the sinkholes and reptilia that abound there. She often swims in the cold, clear springs above the openings to fathomless caves. These are the settings for her Luanne Fogarty mystery series (*Deep Water Death, Dive Deep and Deadly, Cold Water Corpse, Bilge Water Bones, High Water Hellion, Green Water Ghost*) and for her literary novel, *River Whispers*.

After graduating from Florida State University, Glynn worked as a decoder/translator for the National Security Agency in D.C., then moved to Los Angeles where she taught writing and literature and earned an MA in linguistics. After many years of traveling back to Florida twice a year, she has now moved there and writes full time.

Visit Glynn Marsh Alam at www.glynnmarshalam.com.